Red Shirts
&
Amber

For Melissa, who made a boat in my
coffee and photographed
herself with a snowman.
From Bryan Williams

Titles by this author

Chaya's Moonlight Mission
Heliotrope & Hansie
Red Shirts & Amber

Red Shirts
&
Amber

Bryan Williams

**Borrowed
Lady Books**

ISBN 978-0-9560431-2-2

Printed and bound in the UK by
CPI Group (UK) Ltd, Croydon, CR0 4YY

First published in 2015 by

Borrowed Lady Books
31 Stevens Lane, Breaston, Derby, Derbyshire DE72 3BU

For Hazel, Melissa, the Beths and Zara

Contents

Chapter One

Sketching On The Orient Express

The train, golden eyes in every carriage, sped through the night, its windows rattling like the pans in a Gypsy caravan. The causeway from Singapore was well behind: this Orient Express was very oriental; the one to Istanbul might be better termed the Levant Express. Ophelia had made her way to the dining car, where the seats were upholstered in red, with white antimacassars. She had her sketching pad with her and, despite the artificial light, felt impelled to draw while waiting for her sister.

A man two tables down caught her eye. He was dark, not very well shaven, thirty-five to her, though her mother would probably have thought him younger. His face was neither handsome nor ugly but striking, to her eye, at least. She sketched away, so absorbed in her work that she did not realise how intently he was watching her until he stood up, came quickly to her side and looked over her shoulder.

"Very good," he said. "You have my likeness. I should like to buy it."

"Surely not. It's too crude, a first attempt; I could work it in to something better."

"This is what I like. It's so spontaneous. You haven't signed it yet." She did so. He took in her name.

"They call me Mocha Joe."

"What do you call yourself?"

"The same. How much is my likeness worth?"

"It's a good likeness," she fenced. "It's one of my best." She regretted that as soon as she spoke. If he thought she had better work in reserve, he would infer that her name commanded a high price.

"What attracted you to my face?"

"It was in front of me – and it's an interesting face."

"We must decide on a price – and the currency."

This was getting too businesslike. He assumed she was willing to sell. Was she? Probably. Then her sister arrived, which gave her a brief breathing-space.

"This is my sister, Kate," she presented, "and this is Mocha Joe." Kate looked askance that she should have made a new acquaintance so quickly and one with such an odd name.

"He wants to buy my sketch," said Ophelia.

"Mm," considered Kate, clearly looking for an ulterior motive.

"He likes it," explained Ophelia. "He thinks it's a good likeness."

"Can't he look in a mirror? Oh, does he want it to give to someone else? Why not a photograph?"

"This has more character," declared Ophelia proudly.

"It has," agreed Mocha Joe. "She has caught something in me which the camera misses and I didn't know clearly myself. She is explaining me to myself."

Kate studied the drawing sceptically, glancing at Mocha Joe, then back to the drawing. She suspected him of being vain.

"What's he offering?"

"He hasn't said."

Fortunately, this was not Bombay, so there were no plain clothes railway policewomen lying in wait to arrest hawkers. (Boris Johnson would be in his element defending the right to sell saris on ladies-only trains.) They got down to haggling on Kate's part; she did not want her sister to be cheated. The buyer may have been prepared to pay over the odds. None of them knew what a fair price was but, at length, they were satisfied.

"Do you sell many paintings?" he asked.

"I don't paint much. I prefer the immediacy of sketching." Did that sound mature or pompous? Mature, she decided.

"It enables me to record impressions while travelling."

"I hope I've made a good impression."

"I think so," said Ophelia. Kate did not answer. Having finished dining, Mocha Joe carried off his prize to his sleeper, assuming he had a sleeper. The girls could now have their refreshments.

"You ought to look out for people with money and interesting faces," observed Kate as she poured tea. "I don't remember you selling one before."

"He must like my style. I'll treat you when we go shopping. Would you like a Bangkok treat or a Kuala Lumpur treat?"

"I'll have to think about that," said Kate. "We've no idea what the shops will be like. If I see something special in Bangkok – and it's not too expensive – you can buy it for me; otherwise I'll wait until we're back in Kuala Lumpur."

Neither felt like eating much; nor did they feel like making a move. Tea and the movement of the train were soporific as they took in the dining car, the night beyond.

"Singapore was warmer," remarked Kate.

"Singapore in daytime, but it was warmer. Singapore's mainly Chinese. What will Kuala Lumpur be like?"

"Paradise, Emma says, or as near to it as you'll find. Her pupils are thirsting for knowledge – that helps."

"It does," agreed Ophelia, still seeing in her mind's eye the picture that had gone. Where would Emma take them when they returned from Bangkok?

"Is it straightforward," she asked, returning to practical things, "To get off the Orient Express, look around and get on it again? Might they say we should have taken slow trains?"

"They can say what they like," declared Kate. "We have our tickets. There's nothing to say we have to go all the way direct. They should appreciate our custom. There is a recession. Anyway, going to Bangkok first means that Emma will be there to deal with anyone who's awkward, and, if we're tired after sightseeing, we'll be able to take it easy back in Kuala Lumpur."

A sleeping car on such a famous train was a novelty for them; they were not such seasoned travellers as Emma. Sleep was welcome and they did manage to sleep a little, resting with their eyes closed the rest of the time, feeling a slight guilt at not being up and about at first light to see all there was to see of the passing countryside.

"Do they serve alcohol on a train in a Moslem country?" asked Kate.

"How Moslem is it? Do they cater for tourists? And why should you ask?"

"I remember reading about the drinks Somerset Maugham and someone else used to have in Singapore. I missed my chance there."

"Your head will be grateful. It's a good thing one of us doesn't drink."

"I don't drink; hardly. I just believe in trying new experiences."

Ophelia shook her head, with an expression that said: it's lucky that I'm here to keep my sister out of trouble. Kate's expression said: my sister is so naïve; fortunately, I know something of the world.

"Do you only read him for the drinks? Somerset Maugham, I mean."

"Some people read Ian Fleming for the drinks – and the guns – and the sex."

They had half-expected to see their new acquaintance in the dining-car for breakfast and took their time over tea and toast so as not to miss him. From the kitchen came the sound of Western-influenced Hong Kong pop and, more often, Bombay film music.

"When did the train stop?" asked Ophelia.

"It did while you were still asleep, I think. Were you hoping to sell him something else?"

"No...I just wondered where he had gone." Ophelia knitted her brows, then tried to relax and appear unconcerned.

"You should draw the essence of Malaysia and the essence of Thailand and exhibit them side by side."

"No-one would know which was which." She paused for thought. "It might be easier with paint – but wouldn't you have to live in them both for years to tell the difference?"

"Not with your intuition." Ophelia suspected that she was being teased but chose to ignore it, sipping and savouring her tea as though she were a connoisseuse of wine, testing the new offering.

"Here's your model," said Kate.

"Good-morning," he greeted them, sitting down next to Kate.

"We're going to Bangkok," said Kate. "Do you know it?"

"Quite well. Who's meeting you?"

"No-one."

He looked concerned.

"We'll only be there four days, then we'll come back to Kuala Lumpur to meet our cousin. You think we can't look after ourselves?"

"You're very young to be travelling unchaperoned."

"Times have changed." He looked unconvinced. It did not occur to them that he might know about events unfolding in Bangkok.

"You didn't say where you were going."

"No. I didn't." He stirred his coffee thoughtfully. They waited for him to enlighten them. He did not speak.

"Secrets," murmured Kate, half to herself. He smiled.

"Be careful," he advised. "I'm not sure whether I'll stay on the train until Bangkok. I'd better go and get ready."

He glanced at Ophelia's eyes, slightly resentful yet aware she was not entitled to be openly resentful.

"We may meet again sometime," were his last words. And he was gone, abruptly, it seemed.

"We must be too young for him," remarked Kate.

"I thought you didn't like him."

"Not particularly." She still felt chagrined that they should be too young for him.

Bangkok felt too modern yet more comfortable than if it had been backward. Skyscrapers strained towards the heavens like the Tower of Babel, jarring, imposing a uniform language of steel, concrete and glass so long as construction lasts; once the buildings are in use (unless overpriced), national and regional identities can try to reassert themselves. Bangkok, city of monks and naked dancers, neither of which appealed to them.

Once it suggested to Westerners "The King and I"; now there are more modern, seedy associations. Never colonised by Europeans, Thailand was occupied by the Japanese during the second world war. Does that make Thais more friendly to English people? The first English trading post in Thailand was established in the early seventeenth century but was short-lived. Trade with the country does not seem to have been particularly lucrative. Whereabouts was Bruce Lee's first film, "The Big Boss", set? It is about exploited immigrant workers. The river Ciao Phraya flows through Bangkok towards the sea not far away. They imagined coming upriver for the first time when the country was mysterious to Europeans.

"Isn't the heat sticky?" said Kate. "I think we've come at the wrong time of year."

"Would you rather be on the beach?"

"Yes, but we can't change our minds now. We've come to see the city and we're going to see the city."

After taking a look at the overhead railway, which is said to need refurbishment, they travelled by Tube at first, though Ophelia was never at ease underground. Moscow Metro might have left her cold.

"One crowd's like another," she said, "and you can't see anything down here."

Above ground, they felt they were taking in the country, the sound of voices, Thai clothes, the smell of food they might or might not be able to afford (said to be mostly a mixture, not pure traditional Thai cuisine) and they absorbed the temples with decoration both strange and sometimes familiar.

"Isn't the tree of life in knitting patterns?" asked Kate. "Fair Isle pullovers and the like."

"I think so," agreed Ophelia, "but not like this. There was one from Laos on a mug. Do you think they're much the same throughout South-East Asia?"

"Probably. It's interesting that they call it the tree of life in Scotland too." There was a muffled threat from the fleshpots they skirted, like the sound of guns from across the Channel during the first World War.

"I've never had a massage," said Kate. "That would be a novel experience."

Her sister's face was anything but enthusiastic. As though cutting across a corner of Soho, Kate was leading the way past posters they had hitherto avoided. She tried speaking English to a doorman, hopefully suggesting a low price. He seemed not to want her money or her person. Ophelia hung back.

"Would it be a masseur?" she asked.

"More likely a woman."

"I should check."

"All girls. Pretty girls." The doorman found his English.

"And the clients are usually men?"

Kate's eyes were now wary. He grinned.

"We'll leave it for now."

"Massage-parlours," sighed Ophelia, with a shake of her head. Kate was unabashed. An American voice and the sound of music attracted her in to another doorway. The man was modern American size, much fatter than Oliver Hardy in his prime, so he would be looking for food. A cheap place to eat, thought Kate, peeping around a screen... and catching a glimpse of three naked girls, scarcely older than herself, gyrating listlessly. One of them stopped and made for the wings with tired-looking steps. A woman hit her on the leg with a stick, driving her back on to the stage. Kate's lips pressed harder against each other. The doorman tried to force a ticket on her but she angrily beat it off as if it were a fly.

"What was in there?" asked Ophelia.

"Girls. Naked."

"Oh. Bangkok has some sides that don't suit us," she reminded Kate.

Like most tourists, they kept well away from the business centre, which had been taken over by Red Shirts protesting against the government. Red in honour of Garibaldi, leading his men from Sicily, up the toe of Italy (and seeing the spoils fall to Cavour) or as the colour of communism, though Mao's China was known for drabness? There was more colour in Tibet under the Dalai Lama, hard as life was. The protestors were supplied with food and water (and other drinks?), presumably by opposition politicians. According to the foreign media, their power base was in the countryside, which sounds suspiciously like the communist strategy of intimidating villagers and attacking police stations and railways, as in Nepal and north-east India. Insults to the royal family are severely punished by those who have no respect for it, so authoritarian is Thai politics and so lacking in scruples.

Sticky heat and temples, falling asleep, dog-tired, hazily trying to work out a way to keep the sun out of their eyes, local colour in their eyes, sleeping only fitfully because they were not acclimatised. They had wide-brimmed hats, straw, though they also had canvas. Ophelia had dreamt that gargoyles were dancing on their pedestals, a guide was explaining the difference in style between cathedrals and Buddhist temples but styles varied from time to time, from country to country. The gargoyles danced around the guide.

"I'm templed out," said Kate on the fourth day. "I know they're not all the same but they seem to be after a while."

A scholar would have been fascinated by the nuances of decoration and ritual but that was not for the layman. Is Tibetan Buddhism more inclined to asceticism than Thai because of the severe climate? Festivals are presumably more of a relief in Tibet.

"Escalators are the same wherever you go," declared Ophelia. "I prefer the bazaars to the department stores."

"I do," agreed Kate. "You don't come to Bangkok just to shop for Western things in Western style shops. Does Bangkok have a Left Bank? You ought to know."

"I'm not well up in Thai painting. We were right to steer clear of the traditional Thai drama – and the kickboxing."

They were drawn to the houses on stilts on the canals, where people lived as Dyaks did in Sarawak or people in lakeside villages in Switzerland ten or fifteen thousand years ago. The houses of the poor were being swept away to make room for skyscrapers as in China's cities. Would these canals, when drained, provide adequate foundations? The canalside dwellings had not the splendour of Venice or Bruges but they did have a charm that came from the homely friendliness of their occupants, from another world maybe but welcoming in to that world. Ophelia's fingers itched to record this. Did they respect her curiosity more than that of a tourist taking snapshots? She wanted their way of life to continue because they seemed to be happy, poor as they were. Did money from tourism filter down in the south, though not in the north?

They lingered, letting the flavour of the scene soak in to them. Even if they came to Bangkok again and the houses were still there, it would not be the first time. A man politely asked if he could stand behind Ophelia, watching her draw his house. When she had finished the sketch, she handed it to him, saying:

"For you," and gesturing to make herself clear. Beaming, he insisted on giving them some bananas and called to his family and neighbours to admire the picture. They parted friends.

When Ophelia saw the protestors – placed to attract television cameras – she thought of the poor she had just seen, who were not destructive. Kate felt this was experience, something to be observed closely.

"What are they protesting about?" asked Ophelia. "And why are they burning tyres? That will increase pollution here."

"They must have grievances."

"I have grievances. I don't set things alight. Why do you want to go closer?"

Ophelia looked at the tyre-burners scornfully, as if they had been Winnie Mandela. Red Shirts, Blackshirts, Brown. She was wearing mint green. People seldom riot wearing mint green.

"They're not even picturesque," complained Ophelia, "Andean Indians are much more colourful."

"But we haven't been to South America, and we're here. They could be important."

Nearer to the city centre, they found a souvenir shop.

"I'll wait for you outside," said Kate, "I'll just take a look over there."

The shop was full of Buddhas, in wood, earthenware – might there be a golden one for the richest customers? Would jade have been considered propitious or ostentatious? She had heard that white is the most prized colour in China, which puzzled her because she did not care for white; blue and green were pretty.

Buddhism was once more widespread in India, then was rolled back by resurgent Hinduism. How long has Thailand been solidly Buddhist? The challenge comes, not so much from other Eastern religions as from Western ways.

She would have liked prints of Thai paintings but nothing caught her eye.

There were cards of the Monkey god (or demigod) escorting a Buddhist monk on pilgrimage from China to India. Monkey was atoning for some transgression. (Stealing the peaches of immortality.) Is the route specified in any version of the tale? There is no mention of their climbing the Himalayas (at least, in the Japanese telling), so they presumably travelled via Burma and, possibly, Thailand. Monkey's two friends were a blend of animal and human long before "The Island of Dr. Moreau". Pigsy became better-looking in the course of his noble mission; a card showed him roughly at the halfway point. Monkey and Hanuman have distinctive personalities. Which is the more ancient? Is Monkey southern Chinese or did several countries share in his invention? Chaucer did not describe such a motley crew.

She bought half a dozen cards picturing their adventures.

How do you weigh an elephant against a Buddha? Some people would say that you can never have too many Buddhas; others would say that you can never have too many elephants. Ophelia was not in a Buddha mood. She chose an elephant of dark brown wood, (ebony perhaps; it can be black or brown) which was comfortable, with a touch of humour, then turned her attention to jewellery, hesitating between tiny green ear-rings and tiny blue. She went for blue, fancying them both but resolutely saving her money for Kuala Lumpur.

She was in even less of a Buddha mood when she left the shop. Where was Kate? She should have come straight back – in to the shop – she was not outside the shop. "Over there," she had said; and Ophelia had thought she was going to buy something. She had been to look in shop windows – or had she? She was not visible through those windows...and most of the goods were outside...and the Red Shirts were so near. Disquiet became certainty.

She felt lonelier by the minute as she walked up and down, looking from a different angle at the place where her sister had disappeared, as though that might bring her back. Asking questions on this side of the square should be safe but, if she spoke to Red Shirts, they might be the very people who had kidnapped Kate. Absentmindedly, Ophelia took out her sketching-pad – and put it away. If the protestors saw her drawing them, they would assume that she was a police spy. It would not help if she were taken hostage too. Was there a British consul nearby? There ought to be an ambassador in a capital city – unless the Foreign Office had been economising. Might there be an ambassador for two or three countries, even half a dozen? She wished she had Palmerston to look after her and rescue Kate with a judicious show of force that let everyone know exactly where they stood (so unlike Obama's arrogance).

She took out the travel guide to Thailand, looking for maps of Bangkok and its environs. Turning the pages reminded her of the day they had bought the guide. They wrestled over the book, enjoying it, matched their efforts to each other, then their mother called them for tea and they went downstairs.

Chapter Two

Between The Showers

Bumping in to Mocha Joe surprised Ophelia and, a moment later, gave her hope. He was the only person in Bangkok she knew – well, just knew – and he might be familiar with the place and people.

"My sister has been kidnapped."

"Here? How long ago?"

"Red Shirts must have grabbed her – over there – she had gone to take a closer look while I was in a shop. I told her to keep away. Did she expect to talk to them in English?"

"She should have stayed with you. Bangkok is a dangerous place at present. I wondered why you were wandering up and down. You've not spoken to the police?"

"Not yet."

"It's best not to. I think I can help. I do business with the Red Shirts. You're sure she hasn'tbeen taken by anyone else?"

"I don't think so. What sort of business?"

He hesitated.

"Their discontent may result in violence."

She looked at him questioningly.

"I sell guns. Now go in to that café and wait for me. I know the people who run it."

A man came up to them from the direction of the café, not the side where Kate had last been seen.

"This is Jim." Jim was ominously tattooed.

"I'll just give him a message." Stepping away, he lowered his voice, then returned to Ophelia as his companion departed.

"I didn't like his tattoos."

"I'm not keen on them. I don't recommend them, especially for someone with your complexion. Jim has his uses though. He looks a bit of a desperado. That impresses people buying guns; I don't look tough enough. "

They had reached the café, where she could see a vacant table.

"I don't deal in drugs," he said suddenly. "Wait here. Try not to worry,"

She did not try very hard. Green tea with a slice of lemon seemed a refreshing drink that might be calming. It crossed her mind that everyone was looking at her, was aware of her anxiety. She sat facing the door, blankly seeing people pass, too introspective to observe them. Two cups of tea she had drunk very slowly. She would have to let their parents know eventually. How long could she put it off? She remembered seeing someone suck the slice of lemon after drinking tea but she did not do so. For a few seconds, she pictured that scene, then Kate being dragged away by her captors. Kate...was in the doorway, beside Mocha Joe...and as Ophelia stood up, Kate took faltering steps forward, her companion seemingly ready to catch her, then broke in to a run those few yards.

"You're safe now," said Ophelia, hugging the kidnap out of her. Ophelia turned to the table, where a cup of cool green tea was waiting, and she put it in her sister's hand. Never had Kate drunk such nectar. Never had she sat in so comfortable a chair. And that was after a few hours.

"Thank you," said Ophelia. "How did you do it?"

"The men who took her were after publicity," said Mocha Joe. "I convinced them that this would be the wrong kind of publicity."

"The train," remembered Kate. "We haven't long. Have we missed it?"

"No," reassured Ophelia. "You've time to finish your drink, then we'll go and pick up our luggage."

Their accommodation had been spartan but clean; it had been safe to leave some bags instead of carrying them all day long.

"I'll see you on to the train," said Mocha Joe, " I'll feel better when you're on your way to your cousin. She'll be there to meet you, won't she?"

"We told her which train we'd be catching."

"Good."

The girls thought he was fussing and he did not seem accustomed to fuss. It was comforting though. He even picked up the heaviest bag on seeing their luggage and had a quick look around the place where they had stayed (as though they were arriving, not leaving, thought Ophelia).

Jim was a man of few words but he essayed a joke.

"There's a rebel band called the Red Drawers. They're a draw to tourists."

They were not sure how to react, so they exchanged glances and looked quizzical. Jim left them at the station but Mocha Joe stayed. As the train pulled away, they saw him standing on the platform, waiting to be sure they had departed safely. Just before he vanished from sight, he turned away.

Ophelia studied Kate's face, guessing at what she was seeing as she gazed at paddy fields.

"It didn't seem like a kidnapping," said Kate suddenly. "It was like having to wait all night at an airport." "

Kate fell silent. They had so much to think about that the train seemed to be going more quickly on its way south.

"Southward-ho!" exclaimed Kate, trying to be jocular. Kate drowsily let the passing countryside wash over her, Thai merging in to Malaysian – was there a change in the polyglot mix of conversation, changing back as a Chinaman passed, Thai, Malay, ticking away, a few minutes sleep, dreaming, half-dreaming? Ophelia put her hand on her sister's arm and left it there. They were going south and soon they would see their cousin. As one, they decided it was time for refreshments. The dining car already felt familiar. When she was being rushed away by her captors, the thought crossed Kate's mind that she ought to have had a distinctive handkerchief, initialled and unlike anyone else's, so that she could drop it and be tracked by it.

She mentioned to Ophelia that she was going to look for some such handkerchiefs.

"You'd need one up each sleeve and in every pocket. Are you planning to be kidnapped again?"

"No. Once was more than enough. I've aged," said Kate glumly.

"You should shake it off. You'll be right as rain in Kuala Lumpur. You've learned to be more careful near political activists. That's gain."

Emma was waiting for them and Kate relaxed in to her arms, feeling as young as the last time she had seen her cousin. Ophelia had stood back, letting her sister go first, but Emma did not notice and wonder why.

Emma wrongfooted them by her first proposal.

"You must see a rubber plantation. It's a two hour drive to Malacca. You'll love it."

"We were going to love Kuala Lumpur," protested Kate. "You said the city was wonderful and, straight away, you're taking us away from it."

"There'll be time to see it at your leisure."

Emma did allow them to dump their luggage at her flat, wash and have a second breakfast before the drive. Someone said there is a more intense green in Uganda than anywhere else; others said that England is greener than anywhere but Ireland. The lushness of Malaya takes some beating.

The plants can be cut for five years on one side, then five on the other. as "Rubber" Ridley found out; previously, heavy-handed tapping had killed them. Orange under the bark, they are decorative even without the red flowers so seldom seen in offices in England.

Seeing the white latex tapped was a reminder of the joy of walking on springy rubber soles, so unlike the recycled Bangladeshi tyres foisted on customers today.

"When latex starts to flow," observed Ophelia, "it's yellowish-cream rather than pure white." Her artist's eye made a note of that. They talked about the rubber plantation, their host telling them about the history of rubber in Malaya, how the first seedlings were smuggled out of Brazil and the British Empire began to compete with the rubber barons of Manaos.

Only on the drive back did Emma ask:

"Did you enjoy Bangkok?"

"Well..." began Kate.

"She was kidnapped," explained Ophelia, "but released a few hours later, so there's no harm done."

Emma looked suspiciously from one to the other.

"Have you told your parents?"

"Not yet. We have to work out how to break it to them."

"You don't want to worry them. You don't want anyone to say you need a chaperone. Kidnapped. Released without ransom. No news. I presume there was no ransom?"

Ophelia shook her head.

"We don't know whether Mocha Joe paid anything. It can't have been much."

"Mocha Joe?"

"We met him on the train."

"He bought Ophelia's sketch of him," informed Kate.

"So he's a patron of the arts. What else is he? What's his profession?"

Ophelia hesitated.

"He sells guns, but I don't think that's his only business. I think he buys and sells antiques."

"You mean, smuggles them? What do you know about him?" asked Emma.

"He likes drawings."

"Of himself. Did it occur to you that he might not have wanted proof that he was travelling on the train?"

It had not occurred to them; now it did.

"He rescued Kate," said Ophelia. "That's what matters."

"So you're forever in debt to someone who's disreputable."

"He looks more respectable than Jim – his friend – well he seems to take orders from him. Jim's tattooed, and he doesn't say much, and he looks tough."

"Joe? Jim?" Mocha Joe and his mukker, Jim. sounded suspicious

24

to Emma. "Either could be an alias."

"If I had a pseudonym," said Ophelia, "I'd choose something more colourful, such as Petroc Trelawney."

By the time they reached Kuala Lumpur, it had started raining.

"They say it seldom rains in Thailand at this time of year," said Kate.

"Do you feel refreshed now? It rains here at four o'clock each day for an hour; that's why it's so lush. It gives a special élan to people in the city."

"I feel like standing out in the rain," said Ophelia.

"Don't," said Emma firmly. "Be careful. Remember the girl in "Pather Panchali"."

"She stayed out in the monsoon?" Emma nodded.

"And died. Now what are you going to wear when you're sitting outside a coffee bar tomorrow – a coffee house," she corrected herself, "and what finery are you keeping for when you go to a party – a soirée. You'll be dressed up anyway. I've told people my pretty cousins are here and I even went so far as to say you were bright, so keep anything particularly foolish for another day."

They went to bed very early after so much travel and were up at dawn, "Coffee house before shopping," said Emma. "I've got to know an old Malay hand."

"A what?"

"An old Malay hand. He did some reporting for British newspapers but he's not so much a journalist as a researcher."

"I've never seen so many street vendors," said Kate. "It was the same yesterday; it can't just be market day."

"By law," said Emma, "people with a fine house can't stop hawkers setting up stalls outside. There's a reason for it. Many old buildings are made of wood and landlords put up a sign saying: "No cooking". It's considered a fire hazard. Tenants who are not allowed to cook have to buy food from street vendors. Much of the city is modern but the government makes allowance for people who live in traditional wooden houses. There used to be a law that foreigners could only buy houses costing more than a certain sum – l think it was seventy thousand pounds, I'm not sure – so cheaper houses were reserved for Malaysians. My flat suits me: it's modern and the building's not a skyscraper."

It was on higher ground, overlooking the centre of the city. The confluence of two rivers marked where the original town had grown up.

Two people were sitting at a table outside Emma's favourite coffee house, a young Malaysian/Chinese woman and a man, lean and fifty. They stood up and came to meet their friend and her cousins.

"Don Homer," introduced Emma, "and this is the school librarian, Dewey; that's her nickname."

"I always wanted to be one at school. I'm an old-fashioned librarian," she remarked. "I like books."

"We do," said Kate. "They're something to wander in, like a foreign country, and you can always come back and see things you'd missed before."

"You'd be good to teach," said Dewey. "You're self-motivated. Many of the pupils in our school are. We have some fine books: up-to-date information, classics for wisdom and a beautifully written new novel which is just right for people learning English. It's entitled "Chaya's Moonlight Mission". You don't judge a library by how many people vote on line. I like to see people reading, not voting. You don't learn anything by voting. Voters have already made up their mind."

They ordered coffee, which Emma stipulated must be pure arabica, not the inferior coffee which Vietnam has been producing in large quantities with aid from the World Bank, thus denying a livelihood to small growers of good coffee.

"Did you go on the overhead railway?" asked Dewey.

"That was the first thing we did."

Speaking in an undertone, Emma started telling Dewey about Kate's mishap, consulting her cousin for details. Dewey shook her head and sighed.

"Did they hurt you?"

"No. Only my feelings – and my dignity. I tried to think only of being rescued. It worried me that they did not even give me a drink of water."

She was retrospectively indignant about that.

"I wonder if you'll ever see Mocha Joe again," mused Emma.

"We gave him your address."

"Thank you."

Ophelia turned to their other companion.

"So you're the old Malay hand?"

"And you're Ophelia?"

"Yes."

"I wasn't always. In another life, I was a researcher for the B.B.C., then I came out here, writing for a local newspaper and occasional pieces for those in London. I'm a two-bit journalist, Allan Whicker writ small. Local knowledge is one of my strengths; the globetrotting big names often lack that. I'm not a man for deadlines and sensation, more the quaint and the colourful."

"Have you seen the place change?"

"Oh, yes."

"For the better?"

"In some ways. It has the old charm though. You're not on a gap year, are you?"

"No. We're taking time out of school."

"You're very young to be travelling unchaperoned."

"Our mother enjoyed Arthur Ransome."

"I'd expect your father to worry."

"He did," interjected Kate, "but he steeled himself."

"It's not all of a piece," said Ophelia as Kate resumed talking to Dewey and Emma. "The minarets are in one time and the skyscrapers in another."

"Don't you get that variation in many modern cities?" He sounded curious, not argumentative.

"I haven't seen many such cities but it seems particularly striking."

"Interesting." They both paused to let the observation sink in.

"It's a long time since I came to the city fresh – though I have been away briefly. I need your eyes to renew my writing."

Ophelia looked slightly embarrassed at what seemed to be praise. Dewey was just explaining that her ancestors had settled in the city long ago.

"I value my Chinese heritage," said Dewey, "and my Malaysian heritage and my English heritage. I'm rich in heritages."

"Here's a curiosity," said Don. "There's an archivist who would like to have the run of your library."

"My library? Why mine?"

"He was evasive about his reasons but I think he can be trusted not to damage your books."

Dewey was silent, thinking it over.

"Do you have early copies of "The Water Margin" and "Monkey"?" asked Don.

"Not very early. We do have some works on the Koran by Pakistani scholars, not Saudis. We have to contend with Saudi cultural imperialism as well as American. We do our best."

"Will he be coming tomorrow?" asked Emma. "I haven't met him, have I?"

"I think he has an invitation. I'll introduce him to you. I first met him in Hong Kong. He can read Chinese, which I can't; I've only a smattering of the spoken language. Maybe he sees Malaysia differently, coming at it from that direction."

"Malaysia hosted the Commonwealth Games before China hosted the Olympic Games," said Dewey proudly, "and we had fewer problems than in Delhi. We even had cricket."

"I saw the final," said Don. "South Africa won the toss and put Australia in with the ball moving about. I think Steve Waugh scored ninety not out in the final out of a hundred and eighty, two hundred and twenty-five runs in the tournament without being dismissed but South Africa still won."

"Do you know Hong Kong well?" asked Ophelia.

"I've been there quite a few times. It seems a heartless place to me; it's probably different if you have friends there. Most people go to Hong Kong to make money; for some it will be an adventure; they want to see exotic places. People fall in love with Kuala Lumpur – unless it's too hot for them or they prefer the wilds of Borneo. I knew someone in Hong Kong who missed the long summer evenings of England; he'd have missed them more here. Everywhere has drawbacks but there's so much to like about Kuala Lumpur."

"I don't remember reading about the Commonwealth Games being held here," said Emma. "When was it?"

"Nineteen ninety-eight," informed Don. "Long before you came here."

"These girls must be hungry after travelling," remarked Emma, "It's not a restaurant but they have snacks: Malaysian, Indian, Chinese. The chef prides himself on having something for every palate."

"I remember an old soldier who had been in catering," reminisced Don. "He said Chinese cuisine was the greatest, more varied and sophisticated than French. Before being captured by the Japanese he was a small arms instructor."

"Not an expert then?"

"As expert as I am. He had to satisfy soldiers – if he had been too bad, there might have been a mutiny. Some people take a dim view of dim sum," conceded Don. "I can take Chinese food but I tend to eat Malaysian or Indian."

"I like Malaysian," said Dewey, loyal to her roots, not her ancestry.

"I have a weakness for the cakes," went on Emma. "It's not quite Vienna but it's moving that way. Kuala Lumpur claims to be the most cosmopolitan place in the world, doesn't it, Don?"

"It may be. Singapore, Istanbul, New York. Whereabouts would London rank now?"

Kate was looking baffled at a menu.

"They even have cupcakes now," enticed Emma.

"I think you deserve a cake after being kidnapped," encouraged Don, "and Ophelia for being so worried. I don't have a sweet tooth, so I'd rather have a pint of beer. Have it ready for me if I'm ever kidnapped." Diplomatically, he spoke quietly in a Moslem country.

"When you've had something to eat," promised Emma, "I'll take you shopping for clothes. Something new to buck you up. You've mainly brought travelling clothes, haven't you?"

"We do have something for a special occasion," said Kate, "but not so special as this."

"I'll be wearing a powder-blue safari suit if anyone's interested," announced Don, "sartorially immaculate."

"Do you go on safari?" asked Ophelia.

"No. I'm not a camper. I like my creature comforts. I've been to Borneo and seen orang-outangs; that's well worth it. Sarawak has more of the old Borneo than Indonesia. It hasn'tbeen plundered to the same extent, denuded of trees for a quick profit on timber; they haven't sold their birthright for a mess of pottage." "There's pressure though," said Emma. "All over the world there is a temptation to exhaust resources. I'm glad it's nowhere near as bad here as in the Amazon basin."

"Is Andy Ashdown coming tomorrow?" asked Dewey.

It seemed to Ophelia that Don's face clouded.

"Almost certainly," after a pause. Emma probably knew but it was Don who replied, thought Ophelia. What was Ashdown to Emma? To Dewey?

"There's going to be a recital," said Emma, changing the subject. "European classical music. I don't know what they'll be playing."

Ophelia hoped that whatever it was would dispel the shadow that Ashdown had cast over the conversation – and might be carried over. She was disliking him already. Kate too sensed something untoward but clothes were foremost in her thoughts.

"I'd come with you," said Dewey, "but I want to put my library straight before a scholar looks at it. I know what I'm going to wear tomorrow."

"It's a pity they don't have musicians here," said Don. "I'd like to have been in Zimmermann's coffee house in Leipzig. Bach used to play there on Fridays from eight pm."

"I thought you liked jazz," observed Emma.

"I do, but I like Bach."

He was knocking his right knuckles against his open fingers, brooding on something yet picturing Zimmermann's, almost hearing Zimmermann's.

Emma led them to a quarter thick with boutiques. She only frequented shops where she could hear herself think. A cursory look in a department store had given them an idea of prices.

"This is one of my favourite shops," declared Emma.

"You have a few favourites."

"I ought to have; I've been here three years. I pride myself on being discerning."

"So does Kate," observed Ophelia.

The shop gloried in fabrics. Emma was a good customer, so they could wrap themselves in silks to their heart's content, then come down to earth. Kate's eyes feasted on the medley of colours. Fashion for fashion's sake left her cold but colour for colour's sake...she exulted in colour more than her sister, more confidently. Are Malaysian clothes the best suited to Malaysian light? In Iran, Turkish clothes are considered of better quality than Chinese. How does taste compare in a Moslem country in south-east Asia with a sizeable Chinese minority? Is China moving inexorably upmarket?

"Now for my Kuala Lumpur gift," reminded Kate.

"Whatever isn't too expensive," stipulated Ophelia.

Emma took them to a florist to buy them each an orchid, fresh from the Cameron Highlands. She chose purple for Kate, white and purple for Ophelia.

"I'd go with those this time. You can wear other colours when you're taking a risk, not meeting new people. "

"Could I have a big, bright corsage?" asked Kate.

"You mean flamboyant?"

"I like the one you have," said Ophelia. "Could I wear mine in my hair?"

Emma tried the effect and approved. A few days earlier, Kate would have been more assertive but she was not feeling herself – and was beginning to suspect that her cousin's more experienced judgment could be relied on.

"Who is the man who's giving the soirée?" asked Kate on the way back to Emma's flat. "What does he do?"

"He's a troubleshooter working for a big company. He flies around the world sorting out problems."

"He would have known just what to do about Kate's corsage."

They left the orchids in water overnight.

Chapter Three

A Troubleshooter's Soiree

The house had a verandah which extended around all sides, carefully tended flowering shrubs and a terrace for al fresco entertainments.

"Richard is welcoming guests indoors. We should go in," said Emma.

"There's Dewey," exclaimed Kate as they entered a hall through which they could see beyond a very big living room, too small for a ballroom, just big enough for a musical recital – and music-stands were already in place but not, as yet, musicians. Dewey had been wearing trousers the day before, as she usually did when working or shopping, but now wore a silk cheongsam, black with a blue and silver pattern which was recognisably Chinese rather than arabesque.

"Good evening," greeted their host, "and these are your cousins?"

"Kate," presented Emma, "and Ophelia."

"There's a touch of poetry." He shook hands with each of them. "I like the comedies and romances myself. You all look very pretty. The musicians have arrived. They usually wait until the interval before they have refreshments but you're welcome to start now."

"Are they professionals?" asked Kate.

"Students; they're very good. I pay them to play here; it's pocket money to help them through their studies."

"What are they going to play?" asked Ophelia.

"Prokoviev, Fauré and Chopin. Emma said you are an artist."

"I draw. I don't paint so much."

"Play to your strengths."

They saw Don arrive as Richard excused himself to greet another guest. Homer nodded appreciatively as he caught sight of them. Ophelia wore white, save for a belt, silk scarf and the orchid in her hair. Kate's dress was a soft red, not deep. Emma wore a light blue dress, not quite as thin as Directory muslin, long enough to protect her legs from the sun. She knew better than to sunbathe in such a climate.

True to his word, Don wore a powder blue safari suit. Ophelia looked him up and down, as though tempted to draw him there and then.

"Do you have drawing moods?" he guessed, "when you are driven?"

"Not quite." She put aside the idea that she was obsessive.

"Draw me," invited Don. "Record the best of me before I'm over the hill. Can you paint Malaysia in my face? Could you imagine the face I'd have if I'd never left England?"

"I draw what I see. I haven't much imagination."

"You must have to interpret what you observe. You might make more of me than Rembrandt would have done."

"You mean, because I'd flatter you? I was going to ask Kate whether she had seen any change in my style since we arrived but she has had other things to think about."

Hearing her name, Kate looked around.

"I've been meaning to ask you (sotto voce) why don't you like Andy Ashdown?"

"He talks over people and he keeps letting slip that he's a trained killer."

"Has he killed anyone lately?" asked Kate.

"No. It's his off-season."

"Emma," mouthed Ophelia.

Don had caught sight of someone.

"I'm sorry to leave you; I'll be back soon."

He wished the musicians well as he passed them. Kate was mingling with the other guests. She eyed the drinks, mostly soft in a Moslem country, but not hard-line soft. Kemal Ataturk and Mohammed All Jinnah would have found something to sustain them.

Ophelia, more shy of strangers, stuck close to Emma at first, looked for neglected Kate, decided Kate was managing well enough, then found herself drinking orange juice beside a smiling, plump woman (plump by Malaysian standards and to a girl).

Just before the recital, Don came to sit next to them.

"There he is," said Don, guiding them with his eyes. The newcomer was about Don's age, relatively thickset.

"James," greeted Don, "here's the girl you're looking for."

James looked confusedly at Ophelia, too young to be a school librarian. "No. Here," said Don, turning towards Dewey, who was some yards away. "Dewey." She was listening to their host. Don beckoned James to follow him.

"James Alldridge," he introduced, "the man I was telling you about."

"Of all the libraries in all the world, you want to see mine."

"You have books – at least, I think you have – mentioning earlier accounts of travels in the region, visiting dignitaries – Marco Polo claimed to have accompanied a princess. I probably can't get closer than three hundred years later but it would record oral tradition."

"I'll see what I can do," said Dewey thoughtfully. "There are collections of documents I've only glanced at."

The recital began with Prokoviev's sonata in D major for flute and piano, which was arranged for violin and piano at David Oistrakh's request; Sviatoslav Richter, who played it with Oistrakh, thought the original version incomparably more beautiful (and it's pretty good, played on the violin). It was followed by Fauré's Fantaisie and a Chopin nocturne. They came fresh to the girls' ears after some days' travelling amid oriental sounds. Ashkenazy said it took him fifteen years to understand Beethoven. How long would it take Malaysians, starting at an earlier age? Prokoviev was born quite far east for a Western composer, though not so far east as Irving Berlin. Some people would have been surprised to hear such toe-tapping rhythms in a flute and piano sonata.

In the 'seventies, they would have had to turn off an electric fan during the recital, the fan so prominent in Satyajit Ray's "The Company"; now the air-conditioning was more sophisticated and quieter. A man appeared in the doorway as the last notes died away, did not look for a seat, apparently chose to observe from a distance. Did he not enjoy the music? He looked English. They had not noticed Richard approaching.

"Which did you enjoy most?"

"Prokoviev," replied Kate instantly.

"Prokoviev," concurred Ophelia. "But I enjoyed the others. The solo flute was beautiful."

"The sonata was composed about the same time as "Cinderella". It's some of his last great music. Stalin wore him down. I'll check what they're playing in the second part; they had not decided last time I talked to them."

He went over to the two musicians, who had paused for a drink, leaving food until later.

"You'll be glad to hear," said Richard on his return, "That there's some more Prokoviev. Before that, "La fille aux cheveux de lin"."

"Debussy?" recalled Opelia.

"Yes. It could have been written for you."

"Mine's going darker."

Debussy began the second half, followed by a bold arrangement of Dowland's "Lacrimae Pavane", several of Prokoviev's "Contes de vieille grand'mère" and, to finish on a popular note, "Annie's Song". The recital had gone down well yet Richard saw tears in the girl's eyes as she took her bow.

"You played very well. Why cry?"

"They're happy tears. I think of my grandmother when I play those pieces. She's alive and...frail but...in good health."

"You must play here again," he invited. "And have something to eat now." Kate headed for the wine which had attracted her attention earlier, loitered nearby, trying to be inconspicuous (not easy in a red dress), then held a glass below her nose, sniffing like an oenologist. A smile waited in Don's eyes for the moment when the tannin caught her throat. Suppressing a cough, she was embarrassed to see that Richard had observed her.

"I don't drink much," she said apologetically."

"I'm glad to hear it. Go easy. Did you enjoy the music?"

"Yes. They're very good."

"I have had a quintet here once. My wife loves Mozart. She's in Australia at present, visiting our son and daughter."

"There's Andy Ashdown," whispered Don in Kate's ear as the man who had been standing in the doorway came over to them. His shirt was ostentatiously open-necked whereas James wore a tie and lightweight suit, as near to English formal attire as might be expected in the tropics.

"I had a meeting," explained Andy.

"With whom?" countered Don.

"Oh, it was about business models in Third World countries and how we, in Europe, can give the benefit of our expertise."

"You have expertise?"

"A fund of it. I'm much in demand. Governments and non-governmental organisations alike value my advice."

"I must remember to ask you for some."

"Kate, I meant to ask you," said Richard. "Have you got over your scare? Emma told me you had been kidnapped by Red Shirts in Bangkok."

"I'm feeling better now."

"Good. That's reassuring. You must excuse me for a few minutes. Two of my colleagues are leaving."

"Kidnapped?" overheard Ashdown.

"Only for a few hours," clarified Kate.

"You need to know how to deal with these people," said Ashdown. "I think..."

"They would never have dared kidnap me."

"I..."

"Some people know how to talk to them. With my experience, I command respect. I've negotiated in every trouble-spot you could name: the Balkans, Iraq, Afghanistan, Sri Lanka, Kashmir, Libya..."

"Colombia?" interjected Don.

"Somalia. I'm an all-points-of-the-compass man. I'd have known how to placate Red Shirts, give them what they want."

"Are you the government of Thailand then?" burst out Kate before remembering that she should be diplomatic.

"There are ways to smooth things over which we experienced negotiators know."

So he claimed to be a smoothie as well as a trained killer.

"I thought you weren't in the diplomatic corps." Don made a show of being perplexed.

"Not officially, but I'm available at need."

Kate was eased away by her sister.

"You'd better not argue with a trained killer. We want you to survive."

"He tried to make me feel it was my fault."

Andy was soon holding forth on one of his pet topics, the need for multi-lateralism.

"Malaysia can't protect its forests without concerted action to promote sustainability. The pall of smoke over Indonesia is everyone's business. There must be conferences, working groups to report back."

Kate noticed that Dewey and James were in earnest colloquy. What about? She sidled closer.

"I was uneasy on the 'plane," James was saying. "There were two men who looked to me as though they could have been Chinese gangsters – perhaps only private investigators – but that's still disturbing because they kept close to me on the way to the airport, boarded my 'plane and still looked to be keeping an eye on me after my arrival. Of course, they may have been following someone else or I may have imagined it. It was all probably innocent."

It did not sound so to Kate. What did Dewey make of it?

"You could have taken a détour to see whether they followed you."

"I did. I visited a rubber plantation."

He was more concerned than he was letting on, thought Kate.

"There was no sign of those two but another man went wherever I did."

"Followed by a gum-shoe on a rubber plantation," quipped Don. He then went out of the room abruptly. They looked after him, at each other, then Dewey spoke.

"You're probably agitated by the excitement of your research. Is some academic likely to steal your thunder?"

By Alldridge's face, he had not thought of that one.

After the recital, Don Homer seized the opportunity to play Sinatra records, to which the guests could dance if they felt in the mood.

Ophelia examined the records he had brought back with the record-player. "There's more to Sinatra than "My Way",'' said Don, "and there's more to Bing Crosby than "White Christmas"."

"My Way"? I know "White Christmas"."

"That's a relief. His "Ol' Man River" is light and bouncy, unlike anyone else's."

Kate was in two minds whether to demand a re-match with Andy. Meanwhile she felt the pull of Sinatra.

"Is that crooning?"

"No. It's not what I call crooning. I do have early records which are nearer to what you're thinking about. "I couldn't sleep a wink last night". And there's Bing Crosby's "Where the blue of the night meets the gold of the day"; that's crooning of the highest class."

"Does "You make me feel so young" make you feel young?"

"Younger."

"I haven't seen that before," said Dewey, picking up an L.P. with its big, informative cover. "You have him on C.D.s as well, don't you?"

"Most of them. They're not just collector's pieces; he's still popular."

"With me, he is. I'm a standards sort of a girl. Sinatra's more my generation than my generation is but, then, I don't think books are outmoded."

"We like old films too," confided Don to Ophelia.

"I haven't seen many," she regretted. "You mean black-and-white, don't you?"

"And early colour. Most good films were in black-and-white up to 1960."

Richard had induced Emma to take the floor.

"Have you ever waltzed in Vienna?" asked Richard. "I did once. It's an unforgettable experience. I dance with my wife for choice; she's a much better dancer than I am."

The two music students came closer to listen to the records.

"He has wonderful breath control," said the girl.

"So have I," protested the flautist, feeling undervalued. They were eating, so Don held up the record covers for them to read.

"There are several Sinatras, from different times, with the same phrasing but not the same timbre. I enjoy them all. These are singers to listen to; they're not background noise."

"Emma said you like jazz. Do you like jazz singers?"

"Jazzy but not jazz. I like Sara Vaughan but Sinatra is my favourite."

Emma gave way to Dewey, looking around as though she wanted to tempt Don to dance or were content to see him entertaining her cousins. Richard's style called for a bigger dance floor. He was nothing if not enthusiastic. Dewey had a flair for Western dance, it seemed to Ophelia, who doubted her own aptitude. Dewey improvised on waltz, quickstep and foxtrot (slow fox, as the French say), bending prescribed steps to the music. She might have been said to be dancing the Dewey.

"Should I learn to jive?" Kate asked Don.

"Your own generation wouldn't appreciate it and I couldn't keep up with you. The waltz is timeless; that's well worth learning. And the tango is fun."

"You can dance it?"

"After a fashion."

"But you can't teach it?"

"I don't think I'm proficient enough. I might try to teach the rudiments but we've no suitable music. I don't remember Sinatra recording a tango."

"I'm a bit puffed," said Dewey.

"I'm a lot puffed," said Richard.

Andy Ashdown took to the floor as though to a landing craft, masterful gaze and masterful open-necked shirt claiming Dewey as a partner.

"He thinks he's Ray Mears," said Kate scornfully.

"Ray Mears has dignity," objected Ophelia. "He knows how to behave."

Dewey had been putting Richard through his paces but now Ashdown was in charge.

"You'll soon get it right," he condescended.

"I must go and see James," she excused herself. "He doesn't know anyone here"

Andy started waving his arms in the air and kicking out like a footballer trying to reach a ricochet. He then beckoned to the watching Ophelia.

"I like to keep up to date," said Andy, "try my hand at the latest dance craze."

"I'm not one for crazes," said Don with low-key disdain.

"Let your hair down," urged Andy.

"It's down," retorted Ophelia.

"Look out for "Pal Joey," advised Don, trying to ignore Andy, "and there's a song from another film, "One for my baby and one more for the road". It's hard to imagine anyone else singing it."

Richard broke off from dancing with Emma to introduce another guest.

"This is Hazel. She's a longtime visitor." She was indeed.

"I've been to Kuala Lumpur twenty-seven times. It's my favourite place in the world."

"Our cousin, Emma, likes it," said Kate. "We've only just arrived. We spent a few days in Bangkok."

"I don't care for Thais," said Hazel. "I prefer the people here."

"We met a friendly family on a houseboat," said Ophelia, "but it's best to give a wide berth to Red Shirts."

"Have you met the artist?" asked the plump woman, on her way to slow Andy down; on second thoughts, she changed her mind.

"Ophelia," presented Kate.

"I believe she's talented," added Richard.

"I draw. I'd like to be a book illustrator."

"Books are on the way out," declared Andy, taking a break.

"Not if they're of good quality," retorted Kate loyally.

"What I'd love," said Hazel, "is for you to draw scenes of Kuala Lumpur for me to hang around my walls at home."

"I'd like to try," said Ophelia. "You would want something more finished than sketches."

She was turning over in her mind possible materials, sizes, subjects, looking at Hazel the while as though that would suggest the kind of scene Hazel would enjoy.

"If you talk to her about Kuala Lumpur," said Don, "she'll come to understand what the place means to you."

Turning to Ophelia, he added:

"Could you blend Hazel's feelings for the place with a newcomer's? No. That would be..."

"A genius might do it," said Ophelia. "You could make me see things differently."

"I've always liked it here," said Richard. "I'm retiring soon. We plan to live in Australia, near our son and daughter. Andy, while you're still, I was meaning to ask what you think of the border dispute between Thailand and Cambodia, Will it blow up in to a conflagration?"

"They're fighting over ownership of a temple," explained Don to the girls and Hazel.

"I thought temples were meant to bring people together," queried Kate. They're all Buddhists, aren't they?"

"Is Cambodia behind the Red Shirts?" asked Don.

"That's possible," was Richard's opinion. "You would think Cambodians would welcome peace after Pol Pot's massacres."

"Maybe those who would have welcomed peace have been killed," suggested Don.

Cambodia had turned away from the Tree of Life to the way of death.

"Who is Pol Pot?" asked Kate.

"Was Pol Pot. A tinpot dictator but worse because he was a communist, killing in the name of the people, so he got away with much more."

"Between you and me," said Andy, "There's a power struggle in Cambodia as there is in Thailand. It takes experience to read the signs. We have to keep our ear to the ground..." he explained.

"To catch the next earthquake," anticipated Don.

"There is, of course, China, the regional giant," continued Andy. "Western observers study the coded messages in speeches."

"It would help," said Richard, "if they did not keep changing the spelling when transliterating names."

He looked around at the guests.

"I thought Graham would have come."

"Perhaps he had a prior appointment with melancholia," suggested Don.

"Does he suffer from depression?" asked Kate.

"I wouldn't say that. He enjoys melancholy. He loves reading Thomas Hardy. Doesn't he, Emma."

"Yes. Hardy's far and away his favourite writer."

"I thought of him as wanting an active life," said Richard. "He would have liked to be a rubber planter. There's no call for Englishmen to do such jobs now. He told me he would have liked to go with explorers, doing the unskilled work."

"He's having to adapt to a changed world," observed Emma, sympathetically it seemed to Kate.

"There's a place for melancholy," remarked Don. "Do you think it's easier to be happy if you can enjoy sad songs? It gives balance. Trying to be upbeat all the time must be a strain."

Kate wondered if he had one person in mind.

"Is it too late for Graham to find a niche here?" asked Emma.

"Probably. He may try South Africa but never South America. He has got it in to his head that the insects are much worse in South America. I don't know whether that's true." Richard looked around to see if anyone was better informed. "I don't fancy finding out."

"Where's James?" asked Dewey.

"Fraternising," guessed Don.

"I don't want him to feel left out."

She went looking for him and speedily returned, Alldridge protesting that he had enjoyed the songs and the company. Dewey was in a mood to see that he enjoyed himself. She looked inquiringly at Don as he started to gather up his records.

"It's getting late," said Don. "We'd better start clearing up."

"Of course, these songs are dated," said Andy.

"Not to me," objected Dewey. "I must be out-of-date and I'm younger than you."

Regretfully, Dewey let go Alldridge's arm. Kate thought he still looked ill-at-ease despite his professions to the contrary.

"James is staying at the Regent," said Dewey, naming a four star hotel," much cheaper than it would have been in London.

"Is that the old Regent or the new one?" asked Don. "The name's been bought; it's confusing. Neither of them's anything like the Brighton Pavilion."

"The new one's made of white marble," said Hazel, "at least, some of it is."

"Hazel dines at them all to sample them," said Richard.

"Not the Shangri-la. That's too expensive."

"I don't think Andy's been there on expenses," conjectured Don. "Have you. Andy?"

"No." Ashdown looked momentarily downcast at having to admit that he was not important enough to be a guest of the Shangri-la.

"When I first came here," said Don, "I stayed at the Colosseum; I think it had been the journalists' hotel since the end of the second world war. Whichever Regent James is staying at is more comfortable."

"Do you like all of Malaysia?" asked Ophelia of Hazel.

"Everywhere except Kota Bahru. It's up near the Thai border. The atmosphere is so unpleasant. A hotel had been built there with a swimming pool; then they planned to build another swimming pool and segregate men and women."

"The old soldier I met had bitter associations with Kota Bahru," recalled Don. "He had come out to see Malaysia once more. He was captured by the Japanese in Singapore. An intelligence officer had warned that the Japanese could easily land on the east coast of the Malayan peninsula; he predicted that Kota Bahru would be chosen; the military commanders pooh-poohed the idea. He was right. The soldier I talked to recalled going up the peninsula with either fifty rounds per man or, at the most, a hundred. I think it was fifty. Many of the men were raw recruits but he had been a small arms instructor on the North West Frontier. His instinct was to head back through Burma to India. He regretted not having gone north."

The dancer, Helen, and her family did go north from Burma to Bengal. A Japanese officer was kind to them. Her father went missing on the retreat.

"I suppose he had a hard time as a prisoner of war," suggested Richard.

"Yes. He said the northern Japanese were particularly cruel; I think he meant Koreans. But, surprisingly, some guards risked smuggling food and medical supplies to the prisoners."

British commanders had also been complacent in assuming that Malaya was not tank country. They had said that about the Ardennes. The Germans had driven tanks through wooded hills in three days in the summer of 1940; the lesson had not been learned. There were no British tanks in Malaya. To meet the Japanese offensive, they had to improvise. The Japanese had complete air superiority. How many Spitfires or Mosquitoes would have been needed to save Singapore?

Just after the first landing at Gallipoli, Mustafa Kemal's battalion had very little ammunition, no more than ten rounds per man.

"The British don't know," he said. "We'll stand our ground." The bluff worked. It was the first step towards becoming the father of modern Turkey.

"Attaboy, Ataturk!" James Stewart might have said.

James Alidridge took his leave, insisting that he had enjoyed the evening.

"You know where to meet me," said Dewey.

"Can we come too?" asked Kate. 'We'd like to see your library."

"Of course," replied Dewey, happy to show off her books.

"I thought your American friend might have come," Richard remarked to Emma.

" What American friend?" Kate's ears pricked.

"I have numerous friends," fended off Emma. "I'm a friendly person."

As they walked back to Emma's flat, Ophelia had in her head Sinatra singing: "I give myself to you in sweet surrender."

Chapter Four

Dewey's Preserve

"There's Andy talking to Bernstein," remarked Don. "That will be enjoyable."

"Who is he?" asked Kate.

"A C.I.A. man. One of the top agents in Malaysia."

Kate said no more for the present. Don left them to report on a business meeting. The school was closed for the holidays but Dewey had her own keys to the library. Some of the school buildings dated from the 'sixties; others were more recent, low-rise, with a traditional Islamic style courtyard and fountain.

"Marco Polo claims to have sailed from China by way of the Malay Straits," said James, "escorting the seventeen-year-old princess, Kokachin, who was to marry Arghun, the khan of the Levant. He gives a description of Chinese shipbuilding, which is accurate, but he's confused about Java, which he clearly did not visit. He thought Sumatra and Java were one island. Manuscripts differ as to how many people died on the voyage."

"But you think he was telling the truth about escorting the princess?" asked Dewey.

"She sailed from China by that route; it's confirmed by other records. What I want is proof that the Polos were in her entourage."

"Is it more satisfying to draw Chinese characters or Arabic calligraphy?" asked Kate as Ophelia examined those sections of the library.

"Calligraphy, I think. I might change my mind if I saw more."

Books had pride of place here. There were several separate

computer rooms. The girls had seen bigger libraries but never one with such diversity of languages and scripts. As James was leafing through one book, Ophelia, ever attentive to expressions, read satisfaction in his face. She recalled that as they left the library. What was odd was that he had not drawn their attention to the book. He had put it back on the shelf, carefully noting, it seemed, where it was.

Don had dropped in just as they were ready for a break, so they walked together to a nearby coffee-house, not Emma's favourite, but she was absent, shopping. Kate hung close to Don, wanting to say something to him, uncertain how to start. When she did, it was almost in a whisper, so that James and Dewey would not hear.

"I've seen that man before, Bernstein – in Bangkok."

Don stopped, began walking again slowly, so the two were dropping behind a curious Ophelia and the others, then said:

"Where exactly? How?"

"I heard an American and thought we might find Western food that was cheap; only...there were some girls inside dancing, naked."

He frowned at her as if she were improperly dressed herself.

"You went near a strip club! What were you thinking? Were you thinking? You should never have gone within a mile of such a place. I'm disappointed in you. How much older than your sister are you?"

"Eighteen months."

"You should have been looking after her."

"He was ever so mad," reported Kate, still shaken by Don's outburst, so telling because she knew it came from affection.

"You should have told Emma. She understands that you do silly things."

"Do I?"

"Yes."

Don had left Kate chastened and drawn level with James.

"Have you found what you're looking for?"

"Not yet, but I'm hopeful. There's much more to look at this afternoon. Early English language newspapers. I'm more likely to find what I want in a book from a century back recording oral tradition."

At the coffee shop, they got in to conversation about Marco Polo and the romancer, Rustichello, which bits of "The Travels" are written by each, and whether the account is reliable.

As they re-entered the library, Ophelia said to Don:

"I think he has found something but he didn't tell us."

They both watched James carefully while Dewey was more concerned with showing off her library to Kate.

"It's a challenge dealing with so many languages but it makes the job interesting."

"If we leave him to it for a few minutes," proposed Don, "and we listen to Dewey, he'll take notes of whatever it is he found."

That is what seemed to happen, judging by the look of quiet satisfaction on Alldridge's face when they finished their day in the library. This time they headed for Emma's favourite coffee house, where Hazel was talking to Andy Ashdown. Emma soon arrived.

"I've been talking to my American friend," she announced. Her cousins pricked their ears. "He'll be along shortly."

Kate looked at Andy to see how he was taking this.

"Bernstein was asking about your cousins," he informed Emma. "They are said to have met people in Thailand he finds suspicious. I assured him that they're no threat to American security. It's as well they're not Moslems."

"I'm glad you put in a good word for them," said Don, giving Andy his due.

A young man approached, younger than Andy, better-looking than Andy, thought Kate.

"This," introduced Emma, "is George Berson. These are my cousins, Kate and Ophelia, George, and Don Homer, Hazel you've met and Dewey. This is Andy Ashdown, who has a diplomatic finger in many pies – and a business finger, Andy?" she asked, turning to him for confirmation.

"Yes. I'm always promoting trade."

George shook hands with the girls.

"Emma said she had two pretty cousins to entice me here."

"Is Emma not enticing enough?" teased Kate.

"Of course, she is."

As soon as George greeted them, Kate observed:

"You don't sound American."

"Nor does Katherine Hepburn. Are you thinking of New York accents, the Mid-West, the South? I'm from New England; it's the most English part of America."

"Why are you in the Far East?" asked Don. "Did you drift here as I did or have you come here in search of enlightenment?"

"I don't make a big thing of the spiritual side. Local customs do interest me. Angkor Wat means less than the people I see in the street."

"I agree with you there. Monuments can bulk too large in some people's reporting and holiday photographs."

"What about Venice and Rome?" asked Ophelia. "The buildings are still living in their way. Can you separate the people from the place?"

"Not here," said George Berson. "I was working my way around the world, then I arrived here and decided to take a break."

"You couldn't have chosen a better place," said Hazel. "It's so different from Hong Kong. Groups of girls, groups of boys are so quiet. One day half a dozen boys stopped on the other side of the road opposite us and a boy waited for a break in the traffic, then came across and put litter in a bin. When people sit on a terrace in the evening, you could hear a pin drop."

"Have you been to Bhutan?" asked George. "It's a wonderful place, the high point of my travels so far."

"Not yet," said Hazel regretfully.

Don exchanged glances with Ophelia, then came to the point.

"Come clean, James. What you're looking for is not what you said you're looking for."

"That's only true in part, I am doing research on Marco Polo but, for lack of a grant, I've been looking for alternative funding. I heard about Vietnamese Boat People who had left many of their possessions on an island off the Thai coast and never gone back for them. The boat sank; most of them were drowned. One woman and her child spent some time in Kuala Lumpur before settling in Australia. A mutual acquaintance in Hong Kong put me in touch with her. She said that a map made by the captain of the boat had been hidden in a school library. She had briefly had a job in the school. I offered to look for the map and, if I could find the valuables, split them with her. The snag is that Hong Kong gangsters got wind of our undertaking. I hoped they would decide there wasn't enough money involved."

"So it's a treasure hunt," summed up Don.

"I'd like you to come with me," invited James.

"Me?" Don turned over in his mind reasons for his being chosen and reasons for his accepting or declining."

Kate filled the gap in the conversation.

"Could we come?"

"I was coming to that. I'd like you and your sister and cousin to come too."

"Why?" asked Emma.

"Because we'd look like holidaymakers."

"If you're being followed," argued Don, "you could be in danger and so could anyone with you."

"He's not sure he is being followed," pointed out Kate.

"Is Dewey invited?"

"Yes. The more the merrier."

"And Hazel?" He seemed undecided.

"I have engagements," said Andy, much in demand as usual.

"Have you been to Thailand, George?" asked Kate mischievously.

"I've passed through it on the way here. I've only seen Bangkok."

"He'd be more use than us for fighting off Chinese gangsters," suggested Emma.

"I can't come if you're going straight away," said Dewey. "New books will be arriving at the library and I'll be busy the next few days."

"Could I see the map?" asked Don.

"Certainly." He passed it over. "It's a rough sketch, along with instructions."

"In what language?" queried Dewey.

"French. The refugees were anti-communist, some of them Christian."

Don examined the map, finding his French was up to reading most of the notes but not all and passed them on to Emma, the better linguist when reading European languages.

"It's handsome of you to offer us a share of treasure," began Don, "but why should you? And why did the captain of the boat not go back himself?"

"There are so many whys," added Emma.

"He tried to go back but had not yet put together an expedition when he fell ill. Some years later he died."

There was a pause while they all took this in.

At length, Don said: "I'll give it a go."

"We'll come!" cried Kate, impulsive as ever. "Won't we, Emma?"

"I'll come with you to Thailand." Beyond that she was noncommittal.

"We ought to set out the day after tomorrow," said Alldridge. "We'll go to the nearest holiday resort to distract attention in case anyone is following us. I'll book accommodation, then check convenient flights. I'll call at Don's to let you know."

"Which is the nearest resort?" asked Emma. James leaned over, drawing her attention to a point on the map. He took out a second map, of southern, coastal Thailand, indicating with his finger the place he had chosen. Don gave a waiter a wry look, warning him not to come too close.

"We'll let you know," said Emma, glancing at Don and Dewey, "how many of us will be coming."

"Are you walking back to the Regent with that map?" asked Don. "You'd better hide it in a piano."

"What if a Hong Kong gangster disguised himself as a piano-tuner?"

"They haven't your imagination, Kate. Richard has a piano. If you took a taxi, you could drop it off there."

"I'll do that," agreed James.

They watched the scholar-treasure hunter depart, scanning the street for anyone who might be tailing him. Don was first to speak.

"Is James loose tongued? He was playing his cards close to his chest in the library, then information came out in a rush. Once he starts talking, does he say too much? And where has he been talking?"

Dewey was incensed.

"Some people think tomes are tombs. I thought he valued books." She felt he had gained access to her library by a deceit.

"I thought he was sticking his Polo-neck out but he only cares about money."

"When you come back," said Andy, "Hazel will show the girls the sights of Kuala Lumpur. They've only made a flying visit; so has James."

"I'm not sure I could bring myself to show him around," grumbled Hazel, put out at not being thought expedition material. James had lost a knowledgeable cicerone.

"If he doesn't want Hazel, he doesn't want me," declared Dewey firmly.

"We found your library interesting," said Kate, "so the day wasn't entirely wasted."

Dewey's professional pique subsided sufficiently for her to enjoy a meal.

Emma had a question for Don.

"You don't altogether trust James yet you're going on an expedition with him. Why?"

"Journalist's curiosity. I sniff a story, even if it's probably one I can't print. What's your opinion of him, Andy? You boast – have wide experience of business and diplomacy."

"I wouldn't risk much money on him. These scholars can be more practical with their own money than other people's."

"Are we all going to have a share in the treasure as though we were pirates?" asked Kate.

"You're not like a pirate, even on your worst days," objected Emma.

"What tools do we need? Spades?"

Ophelia reminded Don:

"You must sit for your portrait before we go. Early tomorrow, by natural light."

"I suppose so."

Don seemed to be having second thoughts. Ophelia's smile reassured him.

Emma had put her short coat on the back of her chair. When she stood up, George beat her to the coat and held it for her to put her arms in the sleeves. Watching, the others enjoyed his courtesy.

George was staying on the way from the coffee house to Emma's flat.

"I'll call for you in the morning," said George.

"Early," stressed Emma. "We'll drop Ophelia off at Don's, then go shopping."

"Shopping," murmured Kate. It was a murmur without demur.

George smiled farewell to the girls, then gave Emma a longer smile. Kate probed her cousin's feelings.

"Have you known George long? As long as Andy or...I can't remember his name, so he can't be important."

A glance at Emma's face confirmed that he was not important.

"You haven't answered the question."

"Have I known him long? Two months."

"Friendship can develop in two months."

"I know. George is an old-fashioned American. Courtly seems an odd word for someone of his age but it fits him. He's steeped in Henry James and he's like one of James's likeable characters. Have you read Henry James?"

"Yes. "The Portrait of a Lady". I liked it."

"Then you know what I mean."

Kate exchanged meaningful looks with Ophelia. Already, they were dreaming of bridesmaids' dresses.

Ophelia and Don met for their tête a tête which would lead to a head and shoulders. She observed the curios he had accumulated

Don had more photographs than artefacts. His furniture was utilitarian and modern rather than traditional Malaysian such as a man returning to England might take to remind him of the country. His photographs, on the other hand, were evocative of the East, particularly Kuala Lumpur and Singapore. There were also some of Bangkok and Thai beaches, one only of the jungle in Borneo. There was a photograph he had not taken himself of King of Saxony's bird of paradise, which is mainly blue.

"That's beautiful," said Ophelia.

"Resplendent, isn't it? That provides some colour. It's my kind of wild life."

"You like blue, don't you?"

"Ice blue's my favourite colour but I like this."

Some travellers in the East would have collected Samurai swords. Don's walls were not so warlike.

"No antiques."

"I like things to look new."

But he liked classic recordings of jazz.

"This," said Don, "is my second favourite tune, after the Air on a G String, Thelonius Monk's "Round Midnight", played by Miles Davis."

What a responsibility for Ophelia's ears. He also picked out a record of Dave Brubeck and Paul Desmond.

"Do you play an instrument yourself?"

"I pick out tunes on the piano; and I try to play the trumpet. I suppose I'm a pale imitation of Miles Davis but I keep trying. An occasional phrase sounds as I'd like it to."

The artist took up her pencil.

"There is character in your face," said Ophelia.

"I was hoping for nobility. Would you call it weathered?"

"Better than weathered."

"That's encouraging."

"Your lines are interesting," said Ophelia.

"I've seen deeper. Many times," he added defensively, his face open to the scrutiny of a very pretty girl.

"You wanted me to draw you."

"I was foolhardy."

"I'll go easy on your lines," said Ophelia.

"Thank you. I wish wear and tear had done the same."

"Your face is not what people think of as beautiful but, when you think of the experience that has gone in to shaping it, your face is beautiful."

Don considered the compliment.

"Why have you never married?" she asked suddenly. "Did you never meet a woman you liked enough or were there too many you liked?"

"The second, probably."

There was a knock at the door. It was Kate.

"Have you come to chaperone us?" asked Don.

"No. To leave Emma alone with George Berson."

Kate looked around for mementoes of a bachelor existence in the East and settled on a very Western record collection.

"You see the East around you but you listen to the West."

"Music is international," he replied. "And it's not of one time."

"Do you have a photograph of the Duomo to remind you of Florence?"

"I've always liked the shape. I've never been to Florence – only Venice in Italy. I came out East too early to have travelled widely in Europe and, when I've gone back to England, I've mainly seen England, with only short trips to the Continent."

Her curiosity briefly satisfied, Kate busied herself making tea.

"The piano is my favourite instrument," said Don. "I have trumpet days and alto sax days. Sometimes it's chance that decides what I play."

"You've so many records. How do you find time to play them all?"

"I could do with another lifetime."

"In My Own Sweet Way," said Kate. "Is that your philosophy of life?"

"It's Kate's," said Ophelia quickly.

""I could be called quietly nonconformist," mused Don. "I don't make a song and dance about it"

"Audrey. Is that Audrey Hepburn?"

"Probably not. It's little known, that one, but I like it."

"You've opened my ears to new sounds," said Ophelia. (Had she an ear beyond her years?)

"Would you call that cool jazz?"

"Some people would say all jazz is cool but much of it is raucous. This is serene music, I think, not necessarily cerebral. Now this record is by the Quintet of the Hot Club of France, Django Reinhardt and Stéphane Grappelli, great European jazz musicians."

"I think music is the greatest art form. A few books are comparable, Shakespeare, Dickens, but, with these exceptions, it's music that's most important to me. The "Air on a G String" makes the hairs stand up on the back of my neck. "Round Midnight" doesn't quite do that but I have forty-six versions of it. I'll only play you the best. Ophelia liked it at the first hearing."

"And at the second. You've played it twice."

"Come to think of it, my interest in Monk may be intellectual, Bach emotional, which is not altogether what you'd expect from Bach's reputation."

There was a knock at the door. Emma had come to pick them up, still accompanied by George, bearing a hat-box, shoe-box and, balanced on them, a bag suggestive of a new dress or blouse.

"He wouldn't let me carry them," explained Emma. Kate looked teasingly at the chivalrous one.

"A lady should not be a porter," he declared; many in Asia would disagree.

"Now that's what I call drawing," appraised George. "It looks like you, Don. Has she caught your quintessence?"

Don looked from the portrait to Ophelia's eyes.

"It's subtly flattering, isn't it?"

"Not at all," she disclaimed. "It's a portrait of a gentleman. You've worn well, considering."

"Considering what? My slightly dissolute way of life?"

"No. The climate. And worries about your work."

"You're as generous as you're talented. How much shall I pay you for it?"

"Nothing. You've been kind to us and I enjoyed drawing you."

"Let me, at least buy you lunch – and I could give you a Miles Davis record to explore."

"I'd like to have another go with pastel: the colour would give a slightly different flavour if not viewpoint."

"Have you tried ink on silk, like the Japanese artist, Fujita? He's a fine artist. He spent much of his time in Europe and Mexico eighty or ninety years ago."

"The silk sounds expensive but it could be interesting."

"Ophelia's still at the struggling stage," explained Kate.

"Has Don converted you to jazz?" inquired Emma, seeing records strewn on tables and a chair.

"We have an open mind," announced Kate.

"That's about where I am," decided George. "It's better than having an empty mind. I'd like to hear your records sometime, Don, but I'd better be on my way."

He shook hands with each of them in turn.

"Good luck with your expedition," he said, looking at Emma, and, with a nod at Don and the girls which was almost a bow, he took his leave.

"A pleasant young man," remarked Don. "Something occurred to me, Emma. Was the woman who offered to go halves with James the only survivor? There may be one or two others still alive. It's a complication."

"We'll come to that when we have to," replied Emma, clearly in a good mood.

Don took the opportunity to introduce her to Django Reinhardt and Stéphane Grappelli.

"Some people think the violin isn't suited to jazz I disagree." Grappelli made the inimical inimitable.

"I like it. You've only played me Sinatra before."

"Perhaps he thinks you're maturing," suggested Kate.

"I'm a long way ahead of you."

"That's true," seconded Ophelia.

"We'd better be going too," decided Emma. "We'll see you at the coffee house this evening. Will James have made the arrangements by then?"

"I hope so."

The three of them shared out George's boxes and bag.

"You've been stocking up with clothes." observed Kate.

"I've been frugal lately; it's time to splash out. I need to go shopping again tomorrow, for lingerie and beachwear. I couldn't buy them with George."

"He would have enjoyed it," jested Kate.

"We don't know how shy George is," reminded Ophelia.

Emma had to show them her purchases and try them on for their approval before setting off for the coffee house. Hazel was there, still perplexed that anyone should want to leave the city so soon.

"Are you leaving Kuala Lumpur?" she asked, as though they were passing through the Gates of Eden.

James was not there. Don arrived. Dewey arrived. Andy Ashdown. Still no James.

"Has he telephoned you?" asked Emma.

"Not yet."

"You shouldn't pin your hopes on him," warned Dewey.

"Do you trust him?" asked Hazel, who clearly did not.

"I'm not sure."

The girls started talking to Dewey about Emma's new clothes – and her porter.

"What do you think, Andy?" asked Don, wanting a second opinion.

"He could have an ulterior motive," opined Ashdown. "If the treasure were easy to find, he'd keep it for himself. There's another point: are the girls safer here than in Thailand? Bernstein's writ runs there; he has more influence than in Kuala Lumpur."

"You think so? Yet he's officially based in Malaysia – at least, I understood that he was. Your contacts are better than mine."

"There are some sneaky goings on in Thailand."

Emma was now paying attention to them.

"I'm wary of being taken for a patsy," said Don. "If he asked us to defray the costs of the expedition, I'd be out."

"We are paying for ourselves on the trip to Thailand."

"But we're not paying for him."

When James arrived, it was a surprise; they had given up. He held up a brochure and a sheet of typed paper.

"Would you check the hotel to see if it's satisfactory?" he said to Emma, taking her to be the principal judge of accommodation. She passed the brochure to Hazel while she read the arrangements he had proposed for flights and hotel rooms. Alldridge waited for their response. Uncertainly, Ophelia fell to considering her coffee, as though a careful assessment of it would help her think clearly. Kate was keener on the treasure hunt and in no mood to quibble about accommodation.

"We're going for a few days holiday," said Emma, "and we'll see if there's anything in the story of treasure. We can't afford to wait around for weeks."

"Nor can I," replied James, "I'm a penurious scholar." That sort of thing made Don uneasy. Was Alldridge being disingenuous?

"While we're away, Hazel," said Ophelia, "you should choose your very favourite places in Kuala Lumpur and I'll draw them in pastel. I could even experiment in oil crayon. It would help if you could take a photograph of each place. I'd try to draw it from a different angle."

"It's Ophelia's angle," said Kate. "That's individual. She's very good," she added loyally, setting teasing aside.

Dewey and Hazel found time to see tham off at the airport.

"Is Dewey still in high dudgeon?" asked Don, taking Emma aside.

"Not quite, She may forgive him in six months' time – if he's still around." Does anyone still spend a day out watching planes taking off and landing, imagining distant countries, as in Gilbert Bécaud's "Dimanche à Orly" in the 'fifties? Was flying both more exciting and more cosy in the days when Charlie Chan travelled by flying boat? Some had thought that flying boats would solve the problem of noisy airports on the edge of cities but speed was considered more important than quality of life on the ground.

"You haven't changed your mind?" asked Hazel hopefully. "You've seen Thailand and you've seen Kuala Lumpur. Why would you want to go back to Thailand?"

"But we've only seen Bangkok," answered Kate. "We'll see the beaches and the sea this time."

"Don't forget this is Hazel's favourite city," reminded Don. "Are you twice the woman, once you land here, Hazel?"

"Probably, but I'm no mean woman already."

She did not know the city's dark side: suspected terrorists, sometimes detained on flimsy evidence, being taken by Americans to a third country to be interrogated – secret night flights from K. L. to hell. Did the Americans use giant transport 'planes in which prisoners could rattle around – or be kicked around? British intelligence services had colluded in such crimes, officers witnessing torture, while ministers were happy to turn a blind eye. In the late nineteen seventies, Indian women coming to Great Britain to marry were subjected to virginity checks at London airport under a Labour government that denounced racism. Was this Home Office civil servants making their own laws, working slowly towards a police state?

Emma saw a brighter side of the airport, so much more modern than on Hazel's first visit. She was looking forward to a holiday and perhaps meeting someone again in Thailand.

Kate drew Don's attention to a Chinese-looking man sitting a few rows behind James.

"Could he be one of the gangsters?" she whispered.

"Maybe, Can you tell Chinese, Thais and Vietnamese apart?"

She hesitated.

"No."

"I can't always. I'd guess that he's Chinese, with some business in Thailand."

"Whereabouts has James secreted that map?"asked Emma.

"In my inside pocket. I don't trust him to look after it as much as I trust me."

"Did George say he was going to Thailand?" asked Kate innocently.

"Yes. But he's not of our party. He may have other things to do."

"In Thailand? Away from the sea?"

"He may want to see the north. And he passed through Bangkok quickly, as you did. It is possible that he'll call in at the resort. He's a serious person but he enjoys relaxing on a beach."

"Sounds complete to me," remarked Kate.

Chapter Five

In Bikini Mode

Crystal blue the sea, more magical than spurious Mayan crystal skulls; her head was alive and her legs were kicking. She caught a glimpse of the horizon above the waves, then turned back to the electric blue of the shallows, the white sand beyond. Pellucid the water was, not a bit grubby as off the beaches of Spain or Greece, and it was much warmer; there was no cold shock on entering it. Wary of sharks, she had not ventured far from shore but what a deep experience it was to be in the shallows, gingerly touching the ocean with her toes, her fingers, her whole body.

She remembered that salt water exacerbates sunburn. Rising from the water, glancing over her shoulder to see the varying colours again, changing as the sun caught the waves, after a quick wipe with her towel, she took refuge in her barrier cream, soothing and protecting treasures prettier than those in the Great Barrier Reef.

The sea had soaked in to her; the sun had soaked in to her; the barrier cream she renewed was Factor fifty whereas Factor thirty would suffice in Spain. Did she need to lay it on thicker? It was hard to feel energetic in such heat but flopping on one side and staying there would expose the other to the scorching sun. Kate rolled over, sand sticking to her like flour to a rolling-pin. She rolled over again. Might a coat of sand protect her from the sun, sand around cream, or would the abrasion remove the cream? Should Emma have been taken to a more temperate climate to get to know George – well, she knew George, but getting to know him better? They would, of course, have a chastely mature relationship, not being hot-blooded like Juliet or Kate. It was a bit hot to be a man-eater; it was a bit hot to walk far.

Ophelia had only a quick dip in the sea; she preferred to enjoy its colours from a distance, blues, green, black out at sea.

"Your back and shoulders are becoming red," warned Ophelia, who had wrapped herself in a big towel. She came to their rescue, giving special attention to patches of incipient burning.

"Where should I be without you?" asked Kate gratefully, hours of pain narrowly averted.

"George was in the sea too long, wasn't he?"

"I thought so. And he only wore skimpy trunks."

Both had felt slightly embarrassed; George stripped for swimming seemed a sight for Emma, not for them.

The sun, reflected from the sea, can burn though a thin shirt. How did Polynesian voyagers protect themselves?

"You ought to screen your face," advised Ophelia. They had both worn straw hats in Bangkok and Ophelia still had hers ready when she came out of the water.

"Obviously, I want my face to be brown."

She would not have said that a hundred years ago, before a sun tan became a status symbol.

"It never becomes very brown."

"I don't want to look like a Thai; just healthy."

Ophelia was only slightly fairer-skinned and had dark blue eyes; Kate's were blue-grey.

"George's chest is quite hairy, isn't it?" said Kate.

"Yes, though I've seen some much more hairy."

They considered the oddity of men.

"That's a pretty bikini," observed Kate as her cousin approached, probably aware that the girls were appraising her curves more keenly than a man. Had Emma been shy of bathing at the same time as George? Her bikini-top was quartered on the cups, black, yellow, green, fawn. Would she give George no quarter?

Ophelia wore a spray of pearls on her bikini-top, traditional white pearls, undervalued for a time but now making a comeback, her briefs blue. Kate's bikini was the exact shade of green agate.

"I thought she packed a black one-piece suit," recalled Kate. "The bikini's probably new."

George came sauntering down the beach in a blue shirt, matching trousers and straw hat. Ophelia meaningfully looked at his hat, then at Kate.

"I love the ocean," declared George. "Have you ever been scuba diving? It's another world down there."

"We like the shallows," said Kate.

"We try to make the most of this world," added Ophelia. "You're not a deep sea swimmer, are you? Anything could be under you."

"I stick to reefs – there's so much colour and nothing's ever the same."

"Have you always wanted to travel?" asked Kate.

"Yes."

"To anywhere in particular?"

"No. Wherever fate takes me."

The girls were silent for some moments, then Kate inquired:

"Has Kuala Lumpur been one of the better places?"

"Yes."

"And you've met interesting people?"

"Emma has a rich character."

"Rich?" encouraged Ophelia, wanting him to elaborate.

"She has curiosity about Asian culture as well as Western but is not easily swayed by fashion. She has her own way."

"Is it your way?" asked Kate. "Are you compatible?"

"There you have me. I'm not sure what my way is. Am I just another young American looking for himself? Now you two have never lost yourselves, have you? You're both grounded."

"How can you tell that so soon?"

"As the French say, you're at ease in your skin; I can tell as much as that."

"Are you a typical New Englander?" asked Kate. "Or far from typical?"

"It's hard for me to judge. There's something of New England about me."

"Fall in Vermont?"

"I can't take credit for that."

"The Boston Tea Party?"

"I've nothing against tea. I drink it every day here."

"Did you say?" asked Ophelia, "That Bhutan was the most wonderful place you had visited?"

"I may have said that. Until now. The latest place is the freshest."

"Bhutan is far from the sea. You said you love the ocean."

"I was being unfaithful."

"Are you often unfaithful?"

"I wouldn't say that. No."

He sounded more serious, looking towards the sea. Emma came out of the water, looking conscious of her thighs as she approached the young man and her cousins.

"Doesn't it make you feel great?" began the scuba diver.

"It's refreshing," agreed Emma, less enthusiastically. She felt much the same way about the sea as Ophelia: it was enjoyable for a short time.

"You did not show off diving."

"I was diving; you weren't watching."

"He did dive," said Ophelia, "but we don't know how deep he went. He says it's another world."

Emma looked at George curiously, as though that were new to her; she had not yet plumbed the ocean side of his character.

"I like to relax in water," she said. "It's one big bath for me. Have you ever seen photographs of people reading a newspaper while floating on the Dead Sea? I like more exercise than that but not to excess."

"Emma's very active," Kate was quick to say. "When she took us to a rubber plantation, she was rushing us off our feet".

"You don't need to be an Olympic swimmer to enjoy the water," said George. "In fact, you girls probably enjoy it more because they're working towards a goal; they're so serious."

"Good," said Kate. "It must play havoc with your hair, diving. Would you risk banging your head on the board?"

"I'd rather dive in the sea."

"We're going for a walk," said Emma. "We'll be back soon."

"Deserted – that's what we are," complained Kate jokingly, relishing the prospect of a growing friendship between Emma and George. The girls watched them walk off towards the hotel, Emma presumably wanting to change.

"Is George as laid-back as he seems?" asked Kate.

"He's not particularly laid-back," disagreed Ophelia. "He's courteous, smartly dressed – for this climate – he doesn't go overboard in being casual."

"Will George's wanderlust get in the way of Emma's happiness?"

"He did say that the latest place is the freshest. Does he think about women like that?"

Ophelia sounded pessimistic.

"There's Don," said Kate, pointing away from the hotel, where the bay began to curve more noticeably. The beach was not at all crowded and he spotted them straight away.

"Do we look like holidaymakers?" asked Kate.

"Very much so. You're as good a cover as James could hope for. I'm still not convinced that he needs one."

"Where is James?" asked Ophelia. "We haven't seen him since he rushed off when we were half-way through breakfast."

"He's still pursuing his research. I don't know much more than you but he's nearly there – somewhere."

"Are you going to swim, now you're here?" asked Kate.

"Not in the heat of the day. I'll give it a miss. How are George and Emma getting on?"

"Swimmingly," said Kate.

"Swimming together?"

"Not together. One after the other – and after us."

"I used to enjoy the warm water when I came out here but I've always preferred ball games to swimming. When I was a few years older than you, I was on the seashore with a girl – it was a cold northern sea – and she asked me if I wanted to swim or talk. I wanted neither; I just wanted to take it all in. She couldn't understand that."

"I can," said Ophelia, "but I'd probably want to sketch the scene."

"Were you surprised that George turned up here so soon?" asked Kate.

"I expected him a day or two later."

"He's serious, isn't he?" suggested Ophelia.

"He's a serious young man but about Emma? I don't know."

Their faces reflected his doubts. They were both silenced by worries about George. Don looked around the bay and the other bathers with the eye of a journalist on the look-out for copy, taking things in more actively than in his youth.

"Do you like my wideawake hat?" he asked. "I've always wanted to wear one for the name but hesitated in case people thought I was Australian."

"Don't you like Australians?"

"Many of them I like, but it's a point of honour not to be mistaken for an Australian, part of the ritual show of antagonism."

"Is it the hat you were born to wear?" asked Kate.

"I wouldn't say that. I'll probably revert to a straw hat. Have any Chinese been watching you? James's Chinese?"

"No-one has particularly," replied Ophelia. "We've only had a few glances from boys. Emma was here; they'd be looking at her. Won't they be following James? They'd not expect us to have a treasure map in our towels."

"True. He telephoned me, which was odd after all his precautions. Maybe he thinks they're not high-tech gangsters. He arranged to meet me near the hotel in ten minutes' time."

He stood taking in the sea, the girls letting him enjoy it in silence, then he turned with a smile and:

"See you soon."

Hardly had he left the beach than Emma came in to view. She wore a green dress, the colour of her namestone, diaphanous almost to the point of sunburn.

Kate tut-tuted admiringly.

"George would enjoy that," observed Ophelia, "if he were here."

"I see you've changed your bikini," said Kate pointedly.

"I changed after George left," retorted Emma. "Anyway, this is perfectly decent on the beach."

"And sexy," added Kate.

"That too."

"What have you done with George?"

"He had to make a booking for a quick trip to Bangkok."

"When he could have been with you?"

That prompted raised eyebrows.

"He did not see much of it when he made a flying visit."

"They say," said Kate, "that girls dress to please other girls but it's a bit of a waste being sexy for us."

"I was dressing for myself."

"Are you soulmates?" asked Kate.

"You're not old enough to know what a soulmate is and I haven't known George long enough to be sure."

"So it's not a coup de foudre?" Kate sounded disappointed.

"There could be thunderclap enough for me and even for you when you're older – and you'd better be older – but we have to wait and let things take their time." (Like the men Mae West liked.)

"You said George was like one of Henry James's likeable characters," recalled Ophelia. "Ralph Touchett or Caspar Goodwood?"

"Caspar Goodwood when he's in swimming-trunks," suggested Kate.

"Caspar Goodwood might have swum naked," decared Emma. "You haven't thought of the young Lambert Strether."

"Would you? Have thought of him?" Kate felt herself being wily; Emma smiled at their youthful attempts to find her a great love.

"You're nearly wearing Sleeping Beauty turquoise." observed Ophelia. "The sky stone. And you could have worn asparagus turquoise over it. I'm trying to picture it. Would greenish turquoise and blue turquoise work together?"

Turqoise over turqoise, rich yet ethereal.

"A stronger contrast would be better," disagreed Kate.

"I don't think George is so attentive to my underclothes," remarked Emma.

"We're trying to make the most of you." Kate was determined to be helpful.

"Are you expecting to see George again?"

"Yes."

"Dressed like that?"

"I'm wearing much more than you are."

"Has George kissed you yet?"

"That would be telling."

She met Kate's eyes with a smile, enjoying her cousin's for the moment frustrated inquisitiveness.

"Did George rub cream in to your back?"

"I'm saving that pleasure for you."

Emma's riposte briefly silenced Kate.

"You have precious stones on your mind. Are you planning to buy some?" she asked Ophelia.

"When I can afford them."

"Diamonds?"

"No. Diamonds are not what they're cracked up to be – unless they're Russian yellow. They're prettiest as a background to coloured stones. In the right setting, semi-precious stones can look lovely."

"They can," approved Emma. "I'm glad you value colour and workmanship more than pecuniary value."

The girls had picked up their towels and the three were taking a few uncertain steps away from the sea.

"Time for lunch," said the teacher decisively.

Now that she was no longer talking, Ophelia's face clouded.

"What's on your mind?" whispered Kate.

"I was thinking of the airport."

"I thought so."

She took her sister's hand.

"You're happy here."

"Yes. I prefer the beach to Bangkok."

"Let's go and look at shells and coral. You'll enjoy that. Emma, we'd like to look in the shop."

"We've no money on us," objected Emma.

"We can look."

Emma looked from one cousin to the other, then seemed to understand. It was a souvenir shop but with some interesting stock.

"I don't like coral; it's sharp," said Ophelia. "Sea-shells are pretty."

She picked up one which caught her eye. The shell spiralled in to beauty.

"Would you like me to ask them to put it aside?" asked Emma.

"Not now."

The mention of Bangkok reminded them both of an interruption to their journey. There had been a twenty minute flight from Bangkok to the resort; changing planes had made the journey seem longer and more tiring (with more risk of losing luggage.). Emma had been detached from them in the press and had gone through customs first. Don wanted to have a word with James. Kate and Ophelia were ushered in to a room and told by a woman interpreter:

"You are suspected of carrying illegal substances."

And the interpreter left them. Had they been captured by Barbary pirates, the slave market would have been colourful. This was like the scene of an abortion. Some would say that Thai democracy is an abortion, A customs woman, burly for a Thai, seized Ophelia, pushing her towards an inner room. Kate hurried after her sister.

"You're not searching her without my being present," declared Kate, her gerund expressive of outraged civilisation. The woman had no time for niceties. Her fingers were itching within her rubber gloves. Two other women came in to the room.

"Are we the floor show?" grumbled Kate.

Sullenly, they began to undress, then they heard an Englishman's voice outside.

"That's Andy Ashdown," said Kate hopefully. They stopped undressing, daring the customs women to speak. The door opened and the interpreter came in.

"There has been a mistake," she said. "There are no grounds for suspicion."

Spitefully, she opened the door wide while they were still in their bras. Swiftly, the girls donned their clothes and rushed to give Andy a hug.

Outside, Don was looking for them, wondering why they were not still ahead of him.

"They were detained by customs." informed Ashdown.

"Andy came in the nick of time," said Ophelia.

"The knickers of time," emphasised Kate.

"I'll buy you a drink," offered Don, warming to Andy for a change.

"I thought you might need some help," said Andy. "I was talking to a Thai on my steering group and he hinted at what Bernstein was up to. For all we know, he had hidden cameras as well. He's small beer, compared with Lavrenti Beria, but he aspires that way."

"Yet I've seen you talking to him," recalled Kate.

"I have to talk to many people in my line of work. I can't always pick and choose."

"Why the girls?" asked Don. "Any reason beyond personal malice?"

"The C. I. A. sees terrorists and their sympathisers everywhere." (And not only the C. I. A.. American immigration officials were later to detain for questioning for an hour one of the biggest film stars in the world, Shah Rukh Khan.)

"Who was Lavrenti Beria?" asked Ophelia.

"He was a monster, like Heinrich Himmler; he was chief of the secret police in the Soviet Union under Stalin, between the Cheka and the K. G. B. – it may have been the M. V. D. (Don cast his mind back to Soviet initials). I think it became the K. G. B. towards the end of his time or just afterwards. He was shot as soon as Stalin died. I'm sure of that. Even his colleagues loathed him."

Beria buried many a schoolgirl, some, it is said, in his wife's rose garden.

Ophelia was clearly upset beneath her calm.

"Cheer up," said Don. "You're still inviolate – and as sweet as a violet."

"Thailand is so dependent on exports," said Kate, "That you would expect them to want to keep on good terms with foreigners."

"You still have a button undone," whispered Ophelia.

"I should leave it undone as a badge of persecution."

"Once aboard the plane, you'll feel better," reassured Andy. Of course, this was a man who would have relished putting pirates to flight in the South China Sea as a change from bureaucrats and businessmen.

Emma was incensed when she heard what had happened.

"I've a good mind to take it up with the government."

"British or Thai?"

"Thailand exports drugs. Do they think foreigners will bring drugs in to the country and depress the value of their own?"

It was the first time they had seen Emma angry, and not angry as she might be with ill-behaved pupils.

"I think the best thing to do is get on the plane," said Andy, "Then make representations afterwards."

"Will the Thais make them misrepresentations?" asked Don.

He took the girls by the hand, leading them towards the plane, thereby forcing Emma to follow. He saw no point in a confrontation with customs and immigration officials in a country where people can be imprisoned for allegedly insulting a figurehead king.

"I owe you a drink, Andy," promised Don over his shoulder. "The sooner we board the plane, the better."

"I'm always glad to be of service to young ladies."

James was already on the plane. No-one was in a mood to enlighten him about the incident. That first evening, they had hardly paused to unpack before going to see the sea. Ophelia had at first seemed to put Bangkok behind her.

"The sea washes away other people's sins," said Don.

Ophelia's mind was intermittently elsewhere. She picked up a piece of pink coral absentmindedly. It was not her pink; it was not her feel.

"Coral's not a patch on a coral island."

"I thought you didn't like it," remarked Kate, surprised to see it in her sister's hand. One might imagine gaudy tropical fish turning their nose up at pink coral.

"You could have a stone from the Pacific," tempted Emma, picking up a green one. She was not in the mood. The stone from the Pacific fell on stoney ground.

"I quite like uncut amethyst," said Ophelia. "The varied colours and the contours. Coral is so flat, uniform." She had it in for coral.

"Sea colours," she mused, "in amethyst: grey and purple, greys and purples – no, more rock than sea but nearer to the sea when it's uncut."

"One of the five cardinal gemstones," added Emma.

Just outside the hotel, they met Don. He had news written all over him. "Amerigo Vespucci has been at work," said Don. "He thinks there's a code; I like the idea of there being a code – it's fun. The map and instructions left in Dewey's library were intended to be misleading if they fell in to the wrong hands. They have to be studied in conjunction with what he has gleaned from talking to the survivors – there are descendants of other survivors but he hasn't talked to them yet."

He became aware that Ophelia looked downcast and tried to draw a smile from her.

"She's worried about going back through Bangkok airport," explained Kate. "Do the Thais do whatever the C. I. A. tells them to?"

"To some extent. It's threats and bribes together. Pakistan was bullied in to fighting the Taliban. The Pakistan army suffered heavy casualties, which made Musharraf's government unpopular. The Americans then looked for someone more compliant, the Westernised socialist, Benazir Bhutto."

"Remember," said Kate, trying to make light of it. "Wear your best underclothes and look out for lesbians."

"We'll find another way out," promised Don, "even if we have to become Boat People ourselves."

Emma nodded reassuringly.

"Here comes James," said Kate.

James Alldridge looked more confident than they had seen him, neither ill-at-ease in a gathering nor looking over his shoulder for gangsters dogging his tracks.

"Don says you've deciphered a code," said Emma.

"Not exactly a code. I'm homing in on the treasure. Come to my room and I'll explain. We'll have a celebration drink."

"Are you a drinker?" asked Don. He had not bargained for a treasure hunter on a binge.

"In moderation. It's Australian wine, prize-winning. I bought it for an auspicious occasion. I've borrowed enough glasses."

Emma frowned.

"They can have a sip," said Don, "to taste it."

Emma thought, then nodded. She was in loco parentis.

"Tell me when," said James. The girls smiled the level higher.

"I'm not drinking much myself," said Don, "and I'm bigger than you, so I'm not affected so quickly by alcohol."

Slim as they were, they could not argue with that.

"Emma will be missing George," whispered Kate to her sister, whose mind turned from the airport to budding romance.

James would have liked a big table to spread out his documents, conjectures, photographs which might yield a clue; it was almost like seeing the notes building up to his book on Marco Polo.

"What I did not tell you," began James, "is that the captain went back secretly and moved the treasure. He had to do that to find a more secure place."

"What else haven't you told us?" asked Emma. "It sounds as though he intended to double-cross his shipmates-boatmates. Are you going to tell us he took it to Borneo?"

"No." James was a little pained at being doubted.

"Just to the mainland, not far from here."

"There is no treasure," dismissed Emma. "I was always very doubtful."

"Bear with me," asked James, "and I'll tell you soon where exactly the treasure is. I hope I'll be able to tell you tonight."

Emma still looked as though she had come on a wild goose chase despite her better judgement.

"What about the Chinese?" recalled Don.

"They may have lost interest."

"Like me," said Emma darkly.

"You could change your mind."

"We'll soon find out, Emma. You haven't long to wait."

Peacemaker Don seemed a bit puzzled at the friction, being along for fun as much as for anything they might find.

"We'll leave you to carry on researching and we'll eagerly await the results."

He eased Emma away by her arm just in case there were a flare-up.

"It would be funny if he turned out to be a secret agent after all," he said once they were outside. Their own rooms had a different external door from the verandah, which could be thought safer for them and risky for James if gangsters were about.

"He hasn'texplained. The drink was to distract us. Those photographs weren't meant to tell us anything, were they?"

"We haven't been here long, Emma. Give him a day or two."

"Should I read up on Beria?" asked Ophelia.

"Everyone should read up on Beria. There might be a little less nonsense from student politicians. How anyone can be a politician and study is beyond me."

Older politicians talk nonsense too. The ignoramus, David Cameron, thought America was in the second world war in 1940 and the British Empire was not. Philosophy, Politics and Economics are getting Oxford University a bad name. James had come in with a sheaf of papers which he put down. A map fell on the floor. Picking it up, Kate recognised the outline of the coast, the bay, the resort where they were sitting. It was an English language map of the locality. It marked a place not many miles away. What are we waiting for? she thought.

Chapter Six

One Of Kate's Lives

What had got in to Kate's head? A name on a map she had only glimpsed, a name on a signpost, on a bus – if you could call it a bus – and here she was making a brief reconnaissance which was taking her in to failing light. She had not allowed for the bus not only being slow but taking a roundabout route. She had misgivings as soon as she alighted. Near as it was to a busy holiday resort, the place seemed cordoned off from the life of the coast. Had someone tampered with the bus service to deter people from going there? She could not hitchhike back in a strange country (She was under orders not to hitchhike anywhere.) She would have to start walking straight away. A tumbledown building was ahead, flanked by a number of sheds.

Alone in such a deserted place, Kate felt her boldness ebbing. Then a man came out of one of the sheds and came towards her quickly. He looked Thai as far as she could tell. She flinched from the sight of a knife in the Thai's hand, her flinching met by pressure as a hand gripped the small of her back, both her smock and the flesh it covered – and thrust her to the side. The knife just missed her breast, she realised afterwards, unnerved that he should be aiming there. A voice in her ear was reassuring. It spoke in another language to the attacker yet it had spoken to her in English. An arm enfolded her; she could see in the right hand, not far from her body but pointing safely ahead, a gun. She looked up warily, fearing to see danger in the face. It was Mocha Joe.

"Are you going to shoot him?"

"Only if I have to. It would attract attention. And you would not like to see someone shot."

"I'd not like to see me stabbed."

The man had turned tail as they were speaking.

"We'd better go in case he comes back with others."

He hurried her to his car. She was silent for a few moments, then asked;

"Why were you there to save me?"

"I was following you from the resort, wondering where you could be going. I've reason to be suspicious about this place. Does your cousin know you're out here risking your life?"

"No," she admitted, shamefaced. "Are you spying on Americans?"

"How can I be? They're not here."

"You're spying for...?"

"You still insist that I'm spying. You're an insistent girl."

He started the engine, glancing warily back at the buildings, ahead to both sides in case someone was coming to intercept them.

"I'm afraid he would have finished you off by stabbing you in the tummy."

The juxtaposition of stabbing and tummy seemed odd. He seemed to know where they were staying without asking. Did he have anything to do with the men who were following James Alldridge?

"Why did you say Americans?" he asked after a pause.

"I've seen Bernstein and heard a bit about him."

"You should steer clear of him. He's dangerous."

His car was as quiet as might be expected of such a man but Kate's sister and cousin were alert to its approach.

"Mocha Joe," said Ophelia.

"He saved my life," explained Kate.

"Oh, God. Why did you need saving?"

Emma hugged her cousin tight, looking over Kate's shoulder at her saviour.

"I was looking for – I saw James had another map of a place only a bus-ride away – only they're not proper buses with stops, you just get on when you see one. And a man came out of a building and tried to stab me."

"I should pack you off home to your parents," declared Emma.

"That would be unfair to Ophelia."

"You think I should just send you home?"

"Ophelia would miss me. She needs company. I look after her."

"But you can't look after yourself."

"We could keep her safe," said Mocha Joe, "if she doesn't go off alone."

Emma noticed that he had attached himself to the party.

"Why did he try to kill you straight away?" asked Ophelia. "A sexual assault would have been more likely."

Kate turned to the others, indignant.

"My sister thinks he should have been trying to rape me. It's a bit much when your sister wants you raped."

"You must come in for tea," invited Emma. "Was he a watchman?" Her tone was incredulous.

"He must have been under orders to kill any foreigner who stumbled on the place – which could have caused an international incident, unless they hid the body."

Kate felt uncomfortable at so nearly becoming a hidden body.

"It's the C. I. A. base, undercover, of course, but there are Chinese keeping an eye on the place."

"As you are?"

"Yes. I have dealings with the Thai opposition and am watching for signs of American involvement here. Suspects detained by the C. I. A. are believed to be on an island off the coast. The interrogation centre's on the mainland, so Bernstein can distance himself from conditions on the island."

It was no island paradise, a transit house for those being kidnapped and taken away for torture, as slaves in West Africa awaited the ships that would take them to America.

"I suspect," he said, "that the Chinese have been hired to rescue detainees."

Emma waited for him to enlarge on this but he fell silent as if waiting for her to speak. She turned to Kate.

"You went there because you thought he had two maps?"

"He had."

"But the second didn't concern us and the first was less important than the instructions."

Emma tried to weigh up her guest.

"Do you identify with the detainees?"

"I suppose I'm enough of an outsider not to side with the C. I. A.."

"You seem a lot of an outsider to me," observed Emma, passing him a cup of tea.

"I hope," said Mocha Joe, "the Chinese succeed in rescuing them."

"Shall I ask for some food from the dining room?" asked Kate. They had a stove for making tea but no facilities for cooking.

"I don't want to let you out of my sight" answered Emma.

"Are all your rooms on the ground floor?" asked their visitor.

"Yes. These are like self-catering cabins, except for breakfast and an evening meal being provided. There are sandwiches if we arrive back late."

"If Ophelia goes for food, I can keep an eye on her and this apartment at the same time just in case someone is out looking for Kate."

"Have you...business elsewhere," asked Emma, treading gingerly. She did not know how criminal his activities might be.

"You want me to stay?"

"Until our friend, Don, gets back. Perhaps..."

She was unsure whether to ask him to stay the night. He smiled.

"Think it over. Come on, Ophelia. You must be hungry."

"Was there a fight?" asked Emma, once he was out of earshot.

"No. Mocha Joe frightened the man away with his gun."

"And it's in his pocket. I thought so."

"He doesn't kill people unless he has to."

"I prefer someone who just doesn't kill people."

"I think he may know about the treasure."

"Probably. He's well informed. Why was he there to save you? What's he up to?"

"Would you rather have him on our side or against us?"

"What if he's only on his own side?"

"He has helped us twice."

Emma was perplexed, absentmindedly fondling her new pendant, not one the girls had seen in Kuala Lumpur.

"It's me," said Ophelia softly just before knocking. "I've brought enough for five."

Mocha Joe waited in the shadows for Ophelia to enter the apartment, then followed when he felt sure there were no prowlers about. He's a handy man to have in the shadows, thought Kate.

They were soon tucking in to the sandwiches, washed down with tea.

"Pity we can't give you a Mocha coffee in honour of your name," said Emma, hoping he would tell them the origin of his sobriquet. He was not to be drawn.

"I prefer latte."

"Or something stronger?"

"I drink alcohol but in moderation – quite seldom."

He smiled, seemingly aware that Emma was trying to work out whether he was Moslem. Kate frowned at what she thought was clumsy prying. She felt sure that she would have been more subtle about it.

"Is James coming back tonight?" asked Ophelia. "He keeps flitting from one place to another. We've only seen him for a few minutes since we arrived."

"He may be trying to confuse anyone following him," suggested Kate, looking at Mocha Joe. Emma looked at him inquiringly. He smiled.

"Are your Chinese James's Chinese?"

"I'm not well up in Hong Kong gangs."

"So you know they're from Hong Kong?"

"That's the natural inference."

"Will George come to see you tonight?" asked Kate.

"George?" queried Mocha Joe.

"A friend. I think he'll be away for a while."

There was a sound of footsteps.

"Is that you, Don?" asked Emma.

"Yes," he confirmed.

Crossing the threshold, Don looked to Emma for reassurance as he saw the stranger seated beyond her.

"This is Mocha Joe," she began. "He makes a habit of rescuing Kate. He negotiated her release from Red Shirts in Bangkok and he has just saved her from being stabbed."

"Where?"

"He was aiming here." She put her hand to her breast.

"I meant the place in Thailand, not the place on you."

Mocha Joe held forth a map of the district, with the American base marked. He had just circled the hotel. Don paused to take it in.

"She says she saw James with another map leading there," explained Emma. "I'd like our guest to stay the night. I think it only fair that Kate should lend him her spare pyjamas."

"I'm relieved that she doesn't wear a night-dress," he answered gratefully. "But you're not sure you want me to stay. It must be a shock for you."

Her face acknowledged that.

"I'll go now but come back tomorrow. Jim will be keeping a look-out on the road from the base – the girls know Jim. Don't be alarmed if he calls on you in the morning to report any activity."

"Would you like another cup of tea before you go?"

Emma tried to show her gratitude in the way she poured out tea and handed it to him. He looked pleased.

"The girls had an unpleasant experience in Bangkok. They were nearly strip-searched by customs."

Kate and Ophelia looked embarrassed, though less so than if it had not been nearly. Emma continued:

"We think it was on the orders of a C. I. A. man."

"Bernstein."

"You know him?"

"I know of him."

Was it another score to settle? thought Kate. He finished his tea and inclined his head as he gave his hostess the cup. Like George, thought Ophelia, yet not like George.

"Thanks for what you did," said Don, shaking his hand.

"I'll see you all soon," said Mocha Joe as if he enjoyed such unwonted company, and he was gone.

Kate did not look contrite enough for Homer's liking.

"Did I go the right way?"

"You did not go the right way about it."

"I wanted a quick look to see what I could find out."

"You went there without your sister. I thought you were inseparable."

"It might have been dangerous for Ophelia."

"And for you."

She hung her head.

"I'm tempted to spank you," said Don.

"Can I watch?" asked her sister.

"You went to the wrong place, Kate. That map was one James had bought to get to know the district better."

"But there were markings on it."

"He ringed buildings which might possibly have been used, and he may well have marked that as a place to avoid if he had got wind of rumours about it."

Emma's mind was still with their visitor.

"Do you ever shorten his name?"

"No. He might take umbrage. He's not an ordinary Joe."

"I agree with you there."

"I'm expecting James any minute," said Don. "He thinks he's found it."

Sure enough, James arrived without maps but with a revelation.

"I told you these Boat People were mostly Christian. The captain sought help from fellow-Christians rather than Thai Buddhists. Many people in Vietnam call themselves Buddhists but are also communists and Buddhists in South Vietnam rioted during the war. A logging company library was left when the trees had been felled and it was used by holidaymakers and Westerners working in the district. A French lady has been in charge for many years. She grew up in Vietnam, went to France when the communists took over but was drawn back to the East."

"An old Thai hand," commented Don, "or an old Vietnamese hand."

"I have a letter for her," continued James, "from the woman who is going halves with me – with us – and another from the captain to establish our credentials."

"But they did not know they were writing to her."

"The captain did. I knew the letter was intended for her; the problem was locating her."

Kate looked flummoxed, Emma disbelieving.

"Laying false trails, moving the treasure – I'm too straightforward for this."

"You haven't lived in Vietnam under communism."

"Have you written to her?" asked Don.

"Yes, but without giving too much away."

"You seldom do."

"I suggested that we go to see her tomorrow."

"It's moving," said Don approvingly. "We'd better leave you now, Emma. You can get some rest before we close in on the treasure. Is Kate all right?" He looked from one to the other. Kate was not yet her usual self but tried to look resilient. Emma nodded gravely. The two men started a conversation as they were leaving.

"What else do you know about this librarian?"

"Not much. I was told that she had lived in the south of France..."

"Is Mocha Joe your guardian angel?" asked Emma. "He's an odd one."

"He's just the sort Kate would have," suggested Ophelia

"And what would yours be like?"

Ophelia faltered at this.

"I hope I have one..."

"I'm sure you have," said Emma, smiling.

"I think I should go to bed now," decided Kate. "I think the fright's caught up with me,"

"You'll feel refreshed in the morning," said Emma as Kate walked towards her bedroom, just visibly affected by delayed action faintness. Her sister and cousin waited to be sure there was no sound of her falling.

"Kate's going to turn over a new leaf," said Ophelia.

"Mm," mused Emma suspiciously. "Is she always turning over leaves?"

"Not very often. She means it this time."

"Can you tell when your sister means it?"

Ophelia was doubtful, her cousin saw.

"Can Kate tell when she means it?"

"Maybe."

"When did Kate tell you that? Tonight?"

"No."

"So she said it before her latest aberration."

Ophelia hastened to go to bed.

Soon after dawn, there was a knock at the door, quite a loud knock.

"You're the one who likes punching a ball," said Ophelia, "and you like getting in to danger."

So the artist hung back. Emma passed them silently, umbrella clenched in right hand, left fist hovering over the bolt, and asked:

"Who is it?"

"Jim. Are you all right?"

"Yes. Thank you," and she opened the door.

"Slept well?"

"Yes."

"There's been no-one about on the road. It's all clear. Mocha Joe will come to see you later."

"You must have a cup of tea after being up all night."

Jim accepted after a moment's hesitation. Tea was within his remit.

"Green or black?"

"I'm easy."

She passed him a cup.

"It's Keemun China. I brought this."

"Refreshing," he said after the first sip.

"Have you known Mocha Joe long?"

"Quite a few years."

"In Thailand?"

"Yes."

"And in other countries?"

"Here and there."

Finishing his drink, he checked approvingly:

"Keemun China?"

"Yes."

"I'll look out for that."

After he had gone, Emma looked at the girls. perplexed; eventually she voiced her thought:

"Japanese gangsters are tattooed."

"He's not Japanese."

"Do you think he has been a sailor?"

"He may have been many things," conjectured Ophelia.

"Tattoo is Tahitian. Were sailors never tattooed before they came in to contact with Polynesians?"

Wallace, Bougainville and Cook visited Tahiti in 1767, -8, -9. Napoleon and Wellington were born in 1769, Beethoven in 1770. Tahiti entered European consciousness thirty years before Ancient Egypt through descriptions and drawings of its people and flora. Napoleon took scholars and engineers to Egypt; the fruits of their labours were published in twenty volumes. The expedition led to the discovery and deciphering of the Rosetta Stone, which was captured by the British after it had been transcribed. Champollion eventually succeeded in reading hieroglyphs and opening a door to an unknown civilisation.

"Criminals were branded in the Middle Ages," recalled Emma. "Maybe it was black humour, saying they were treated like criminals."

"Tahitians wanted to be works of art," surmised Kate. "Do you think Jim wants to be one? He can't paint like Ophelia but he shows the world what he would paint if he could."

"Jim has two small dragon tattoos," observed Ophelia. "Won't they be Chinese, not Polynesian?"

"I should think so, although Polynesians are believed to have migrated from south China. Have you been studying the patterns?"

"She has an eye for design," explained Kate.

"I think it's a matter of fashion," said Emma, no slave of fashion herself. "Think of footballers and film stars – they never used to be tattooed."

"If he had been a sailor," asked Ophelia, "would you mind so much?"

"No. I'd rather he were a sailor than a gangster."

Emma turned to another point:

"Jim must have knocked about the Far East for years but what is his nationality?"

"He's not American," said Ophelia, "nor Scottish."

"Irish?" hazarded Kate.

"An Englishman who has lived in Australia or New Zealand," seemed as likely as anything to Emma.

"Jim won't tell you his life story," said Kate. "If you knew him ten years, he wouldn't do that."

"He might if he had a few drinks," suggested Ophelia.

"Jim a drinker! Never!"

"You made tea stronger for Jim than for Mocha Joe – or us. Does he look a strong tea type?"

"Yes. I could have given him more water if he had liked it weaker. He looks strong, though he is not particularly brawny. I wonder how much fighting he has done."

"Mocha Joe said it's handy that Jim looks tough," informed Kate helpfully.

"I'd feel more comfortable if he weren't looking tough near me."

"He liked your Keemun China," reminded Ophelia. "He may be a gourmet in disguise."

Emma's expression said: you are being over-imaginative.

"Jim's telling us even less about Mocha Joe than he did himself."

"Don't you trust Mocha Joe?" asked Kate.

"I trust him to look after you but he may intend to look after the treasure. When he followed you, he must already have been watching us. Why are they in the district?"

"Smuggling by sea?" suggested Kate. Ophelia nodded.

"Don must have gone out early, otherwise he would have heard the knock and come to see who was here. We'd better go down to the beach to relax while we're waiting."

"Have we time to bathe?"

"You'd have to hurry. Better to wait until tomorrow. We ought to have a good breakfast. It could be a long drive."

"And a long dig," said Kate.

"I'm not sure whether that's being optimistic or not. I don't feel like digging in this heat."

They had a breakfast which might have been hearty, had their thoughts not been elsewhere and the heat even at that time of day put them off any heavy food.

"I still don't think much of starfruit," declared Ophelia.

"Nor do I," concurred Emma. "And I've tried it more times than you have." The service was as usual good, which had been their experience when officialdom was not involved.

"We may as well have another look at the souvenir shop," said Kate. "You never know what you might find."

The sea looked tempting. Was Emma picturing a bronzed bather?

Kate had hurried ahead as though set on some sale purchase, Ophelia glancing towards the sea as she walked more slowly. She turned at the entrance. Kate's hand was behind her back.

"I thought you'd like this," said Kate, proffering the sea-shell Ophelia had looked at the day before. Her sister smiled at the thought and held the shell up to see if the colours changed.

"Hold it to your ear," urged Kate. "It is said that, if you hold a sea-shell to your ear, you can hear the sound of the sea."

Emma smiled to see Ophelia more cheerful.

"Peridots have been found in meteorites. If you hold a peridot to your ear, can you hear the music of the spheres?"

"Peridots?" asked Kate.

"They're light green; not worth as much as emeralds but still pretty."

"Don's not rich," said Kate, "but he's still quite handsome. There he is."

He was walking along the beach, letting each wave wash over his shoes, not quite to the instep. He smiled sheepishly at being caught in a childish game, then quickly became businesslike. They looked at him expectantly as he neared.

"We've hired a car," said Don, "and James has broken telephone silence to confirm that we're going. I think one of the reasons he wanted you to come is that girls will be reassuring. Madame Sir would have been nervous and suspicious of a strange man."

"That makes sense," acknowledged Emma.

"Given time, we'd understand how his mind works. I've done research, so I should know a bit about researchers. He probably thinks of Marco Polo as his lottery ticket."

"Isn't the treasure that?"

"It's secondary. His hunting instinct is scholarly; he'll take the money but it's to fund his work. Did you have an undisturbed night?"

"Yes, thank you. Jim did call this morning."

"Was he the Jim you expected?"

"I'm afraid so. He was civil enough but I daren't look at his tattoos."

"There may be a naked woman up his sleeve," suggested Kate.

Emma looked at Ophelia for confirmation.

"Probably. He has a peony. That's Chinese, isn't it?"

"For good luck," said Emma. "It's a mercy he hasn't a skull and cross bones."

Don tried to allay Emma's fears:

"Marquesan Islanders were the most extensively tattooed of Polynesians but they were no fiercer than Samoan rugby players."

That was not altogether reassuring. Don tried again:.

"Does he sound Glaswegian?"

"No."

"That's something."

"He has taken a fancy to Keemun China tea," said Kate.

"That would have pleased Jane Austen."

"Is there any point in going to the Thai police about the attack on Kate?"

"I think we'd be wise to steer clear of them. Kate could be accused of trespass; the police could be implicated in the attack; we're associating with people they don't like; and, if we find anything, we may have to smuggle it out of the country. Two lots of Chinese, the Thai police and the C. I. A. watching each other, and we're in the middle – or perhaps on the periphery."

"You said," recalled Ophelia, looking at Emma, "that Polynesians migrated across the Pacific. Why did they not settle in Australia? Aborigines are not Polynesians, are they?"

Emma looked to Don to answer.

"No, they're not. Winds and currents. Keeping out of the way of hostile tribes. It's complicated: Fijians are Melanesian – then Indians arrived. I need a cool drink before I try to explain any more."

"Have you had no breakfast?" asked Emma.

"No. I'll go and ask for some sandwiches and fruit. James will be here quite soon."

"We'll walk along the beach," said Kate. "Are you coming, Emma?"

"Not straight away. I'd like to find gifts for Dewey and Hazel. There may not be much in the souvenir shop but it could give me ideas."

"Give them something from the treasure," said Kate.

"Now that's an idea."

The girls walked farther around the bay than thay had done the previous day, looking back towards the beach from which they had swum. Had the full force of the tsunami hit this bay or had it been dissipated by sheltering land? It looked peaceful now. They took in the picture, knowing they would only see that beach once or twice more.

"Emma will be waiting," said Ophelia. They turned back, cutting close to the water's edge, the sea momentarily tepid on their ankles.

"There's George," cried Kate excitedly. Their cousin had come out of the shop, intending to come to meet them, but had been diverted. They quickened their steps and just caught Emma's opening words.

Chapter Seven

Spinels Galore

"I thought you'd gone."

"Without seeing you?"

"You seemed to be in a hurry."

"There are things I want to see but I'll be hurrying back, especially because of what I heard. I met a friend of yours I didn't know about. He goes by the name of Mocha Joe."

"I didn't know he was my friend. I only know him through my cousins. He has helped them twice."

"I haven't heard the details of that. He did say that they're being treated with suspicion by the C. I. A. because of a misunderstanding. He doesn't give much away. He said he had business in Thailand, then hung fire."

"That's Mocha Joe. He set his employee or accomplice to watch over us."

"I'd like to watch over you myself. I feel a bit guilty going away. I'll give Bangkok twenty-four hours, then devote the rest of my time to you."

"That sounds like devotion," whispered Kate.

"What did you make of Mocha Joe?" asked Emma. "Did you like him?"

"I liked you more when I met you. And you've grown on me. You said he had helped your cousins, so he must have some good in him. You look doubtful."

"I feel wary. I have the girls to think of."

He paused, looking in to her eyes almost absentmindedly. He

seemed to be thinking something over. She guessed.

"Might I kiss you?"

"Of course."

She kissed his hat off. Treading lightly so as not to disturb them, Kate came forward and picked it up from the sand, waiting silently for the two to part.

"George, your hat."

"Thank you."

He waved his hat airily as he bowed, not ostentatiously, but going beyond a nod. His mood was in his hat. He smiled at the girls as he walked off.

"His hat might have blown away," explained Kate.

"Thoughtful of you. Was the kiss worth waiting for?"

"Yes. Romantic," approved Ophelia.

Emma seemed to be carried on a sunbeam back to the hotel, her cousins lagging behind reviewing the scene.

"We'll have to keep Emma on the straight and narrow," joked Kate.

"I thought she was keeping us on the straight and narrow."

Emma seemed undecided whether to dress to impress a French lady or for a long dusty journey.

"Casual smart," suggested Kate.

"That's not much help."

"The cream silk," said Ophelia. "George likes it."

"Did he say so?"

"He didn't need to."

A knock interrupted their deliberations. Opening the door expecting to see Don, Emma was greeted by Mocha Joe.

"Did Jim turn up?"

"Yes."

"And there were no prowlers?"

"No. The girls told me a little about him. I feel intimidated by him. There's an alien way of life cut in to his skin."

"You get used to it. His tattoos are only skin-deep."

"What's deeper?"

"Not much as far as we can tell. He has his good points. He's loyal."

"To you?"

"I hope so."

"The Hong Kong gangsters – they are not loyal to you, are they? Or you to them? They're not giving orders to you?"

"I don't take orders. It depends which gangsters you mean. It's hard to keep track of them, even if you've made a special study of the subject. I saw James outside parking, driving out and parking again."

"He's getting used to a hired car."

"Enjoy your drive," he said, glancing at the two flasks of hot coffee and the fruit waiting to be packed.

"Thank you. Is there any reason we shouldn't?"

"Not at present."

"So we don't need to be wary?"

"Not today." He left smiling at them. Was he also smiling to himself at what he knew?

"I think you're right, Ophelia," decided Emma. She put on the cream silk dress, buttoned all the way down the front, and took out a shawl and an antique scarf such as Isabelle Adjani collects.

"The scarf," excaimed Kate. "It adds a splash of colour."

"It does," agreed Ophelia.

The girls wore pastel-coloured trousers, not ubiquitous jeans, ready for an upmarket archaelogical excavation.

"Are you ready?" asked Don through the door as he knocked.

"Yes," called Emma, picking up a basket. The girls had smaller bags, so they should have provisions to last through the return journey. James was outside, at the wheel and looking confident with nearness to his objective.

"How do we approach her?" asked Emma. "Have you brought your bona fides?"

"I have signatures she can check, circumstantial evidence."

"The girls have honest faces," said Don. "You're asking a lot if the treasure is worth much. She has to trust you."

"There are people in Hong Kong to vouch for me and in Australia – and beyond the grave."

"If she takes to you, you're all right," said Emma. "If she doesn't..."

After an hour and a half, they came to a small town, which may once have been close to forest but that was long gone. James drove slowly, stopping once to check the directions he had written down. Turning a corner, they saw a brick building set apart. Madame Sir was sitting on the verandah, looking out for them. She was grey-haired, smart in dress and matching jacket between purple and magenta. The car stopped.

"Mr. Alldridge?" she inquired.

"Madame Sir?" She nodded, taking in his companions with a friendly look.

He opened a document case, containing letters, both old and recent.

"We had better go to my office. You won't drop them."

She led the way through the library, which was closed that afternoon, to a small but tastefully furnished office – the sort a librarian of the old school naturally has. The scent of flowers was not too heavy.

She took out letters sent to her in the past, comparing the handwriting. She looked satisfied, relieved.

"It's a weight off my shoulders. I did not know what to put in my testament if no-one came to claim it soon. Would you like a glass of wine?"

"You keep wine in your office? Very French."

"You know France?"

"Not so well as I know ex-patriate French. I've been out here a long time."

"You too are drawn to the East?"

"Yes." He nodded.

"I have two bottles left from my département. I still have one, although this has long been my home."

She handed glasses of wine to the three adults, then gave a little less to the girls, Don passing on their glasses with the comment:

"Twice in twenty-four hours – you're in luck."

"We don't enjoy it yet though," qualified Ophelia.

"Don't try too hard. You don't have to like it. If you're going to, it will come. Savour quality in small measure."

Turning to Madame Sir, he asked: "Was that unFrench?"

"No. It was good advice."

Kate was getting the hang of sniffing wine, keeping it on her tongue for an age, then regretfully swallowing as though saying goodbye to an old friend. Madame Sir waited for them all to finish before saying:

"I've made an inventory of the cache. I keep checking the condition of the books and manuscripts."

"Books?"

"They are rare – with more than sentimental value."

She led the way to the book store. As some people have fake books hiding a drinks cabinet, she had real books hiding jewels. She was as careful with her best books as with precious stones and figurines.

"You must help me move these." Books were piled on top of a box of books, with others at right angles.

"It has kept me fit moving these whenever I've checked..." She was still discreet.

They formed a chain as though passing buckets of water to put a fire out. A wooden chest was disclosed behind; it smelt of mahogany. Madame Sir took out a key and inserted it in the lock.

"Is it stiff?" asked Don.

"A little." But she had the knack and the key turned. She raised the lid. Gems were protruding from bags, probably hessian. She picked up one bag and took out a jade figurine, white, surely of a goddess. She handed that to James, the most knowledgeable about Chinese and Indo-Chinese art. Then she took out a book, opening it at photographs of old Saigon, French and Vietnamese.

"This," she said fondly, "is for a bibliophile."

"We have a friend who is a librarian," said Emma.

There was a necklace of assorted animals: monkeys, leopards, elephants, another of Eastern goddesses, clothed and otherwise.

"I like your scarf," complimented Madame Sir. "It's pretty by any light."

"Thank you." It showed a doe escaping from hunters while its fawn lay in hiding.

"What are those dark stones?"

"Spinels," said Madame Sir.

"I thought they were like rubies and it was hard to tell them apart until well into the nineteenth century."

"You don't know where you are with gemstones sometimes. A few per cent of sapphires are pink."

"Spinels galore!" exclaimed Don as she opened another bag, overflowing with gems, a few of them pale green.

"Peridots," guessed Ophelia.

"Probably," said Emma, looking to Madame Sir for confirmation.

"I think so. There are pearls, both white and Tahitian, and..." She pulled a hessian bag out of another. "Sapphires. Small but sapphires."

She unrolled a painting and handed it to Emma, who passed it on to Ophelia. It was of a street scene in Saigon, with a slight Renoir influence. There was more jade, this time a saintly-looking sage and, separately, a leopard. Madame Sir paused on unrolling a second painting, a full-length portrait of a woman in oriental dress, most likely Vietnamese or Chinese.

"Do you know her?" asked Emma.

"No, but it's a reminder of old Saigon. Communist or capitalist, they'd dress differently now."

They had emptied all the bags and were able to take stock of the hoard: three books, a manuscript, two paintings, jade figurines and a piece of uncarved jade, and numerous gemstones. Ophelia was examining the first painting. .

"She's an artist," informed Kate.

"I should like to see your work."

"Better still, I'll draw you," ventured Ophelia, emboldened by the occasion. "My sketch-book is in the car."

"Would you like to come to my house for coffee?" invited Madame Sir.

"We'd be delighted," accepted Emma.

"I'll go and unlock the door for Ophelia," said James.

"She never goes far without her sketch-book," explained Kate, adding when her sister was out of earshot: "She's diffident until she gets a chance to draw."

"I can give you some hessian bags," said Madame Sir, "and some books for concealment. I'll be running down my stocks but I shall not be here much longer." She threw a dust-sheet over the hoard, then locked the store-room door. "What better place to hide treasure than in a library?" mused Don. "What better place to find treasure?"

The house was only a few hundred yards away. There was a sandalwood scented candle, unlit. Around the walls and on a small table were photographs of Saigon and of what looked like a Mediterranean seafront. There was also a painting of a French or Italian street scene. Emma studied the pictures.

"Do you miss France?"

"Sometimes. But I chose my path. I belong in the Far East; or did. It is almost time to retire. Then I can rediscover my other country."

"That looks like the south," observed Emma. "Did you live in Provence?"

"West of Provence. The département of Hérault, between the Pyrenees and the Mediterranean."

She made coffee for them and offered them biscuits, Italian and Belgian; but her records were French: Charles Trenet and Aznavour to join her divided heart.

"Emmenez-moi au bout de la terre, Emmenez-moi au pays de merveilles," sang Aznavour. Madame Sir had not gone quite to the end of the earth.

"Was Vietnam a land of marvels for you?" asked Emma.

"I was young. Much of it was strange and marvelous. Southern France has its charms. Perhaps, when I retire, I shall learn to appreciate it more than the country so near yet so far away."

They listened to the beautiful "Hier encore, j'avais vingt ans". With Aznavour in her ears, Ophelia dashed off a sketch of Madame Sir.

"That's inspired," said Don. "It's the Armenian influence."

Kate had made a round of the photographs, comparing Saigon of the nineteen sixties with what she had seen in present-day Malaysia and Thailand.

"Could you have gone back to Vietnam when the storm blew over?"

"No. It will never be the same."

"It was a big storm," added Don.

"What was the war about?" asked Kate, too young to know the reverberations of her question.

"Shall I?" asked Don. Madame Sir nodded.

"The communist north invaded the south, infiltrating towns and villages, and claiming it was a war of liberation from colonialism. The Americans tried to win by indiscriminate bombing, which played in to the hands of communist propagandists. Atrocities committed by the communists were seldom mentioned on American television news. Hue..."

"Why I could not go back," explained Madame Sir. At Hue, the Vietcong, egged on by Marxist university lecturers, massacred hundreds of educated people.

"I thought you came to Thailand, hoping to go back," said Emma.

"An illusion," replied Madame Sir sadly. "Perhaps I should have made a clean break. I had begun a new life in France. How could I hope to pick up where I had left off in Saigon?"

She finished her coffee slowly, the only sound for the moment the voice of an immigrant. Trying to divert her thoughts, Don asked:

"Do you miss hearing French?"

"Yes. Sometimes I talk to holidaymakers."

Her namesake, Gérard Sir, said:

"The Languedoc is the paradise of the French language."

Ophelia finished her sketch and pressed it in to their hostess's hands. The Frenchwoman smiled, curious at seeing herself through someone else's eyes.

"George said: 'You can't live everywhere'," said Emma.

"He has done his best to," remarked Don.

"Has he seen enough of the world yet?" asked Kate.

"I don't know." Emma was pensive, hopeful not anxious.

"Are we going to take everything today?" asked James.

"I'm going by Mocha Joe," said Emma. "If he thinks it's safe today, we should take it today; he may not know about tomorrow."

"You trust him?"

"Up to a point."

"We can't hire an armoured car," said Don. "We have to take a chance – and he has helped the girls. He may plan to rob us; more likely he's preoccupied with other things."

As Madame Sir put the CD away, he asked:

"Isn't Georges Brassens from your region?"

"My département. He was born at Sète, He is not one of my favourites because he uses gross language at times but he is a poet. I disapprove of him and at the same time I'm proud of him."

Emma sniffed the sandalwood.

"Soon I shall be sniffing lavender," continued Madame Sir, " but that will always be a reminder of the East. I shall keep sandalwood by me."

Aznavour said: "They are with me from twelve until death," so the girls had come in to his orbit.

"You said he's Armenian," Ophelia quizzed Don.

"He was born in France but I think his parents had only lately arrived. He used to go out with a brief-case selling songs. I read that he only started singing because he could not persuade others to sing his songs but that may not be accurate. You can't always trust journalists or record covers – and that's from a journalist."

That "voilé", veiled voice stayed with them as they repaired to the store-room. Thinking to empty the contents of one bag into another, Don tipped out a coin, which he examined before replacing it where he had found it.

"Does Hazel have a Napoleon?"

"No." Emma shook her head.

"She likes gold," he explained.

"Not only gold," Emma clarified. "She likes pretty jewellery, not too heavy."

They filled a number of hessian bags and Madame Sir selected books that could be used to cover them.

"You ought to keep something for yourself," urged James, "from my share, so you won't be depriving anyone."

"No. That would not be right. I have Ophelia's drawing; that is enough for me."

Ophelia had a rolled-up painting down each leg of her trousers so that she would not have one fat leg and one thin thus arousing suspicion.

"But you won't be walking far with them," pointed out Kate.

"Never mind. I'm showing initiative."

"She's not just a pretty face and a ready pencil," said Don.

They carried all the bags and books out, putting the latter on the back seat while they thought. James opened the boot and closed it again.

"Do you think it's not safe too?" asked Emma. "I feel that someone could open the boot as soon as we stop. All this is worth much more than I expected."

"We'd better put it inside," agreed Don. Madame Sir hugged Emma and the girls while the two men stood a little apart.

"May the Languedoc feel like home," wished Don. They waved to the librarian as the engine jerked in to life.

"You do have room to handle the steering wheel?" checked Emma.

There were bags by the driver's feet, Don's, and, lighter, on their laps, covered with books.

"I think there's more weight in the books," complained Kate, adjusting them on to the seat, with gemstones still concealed.

They had been driving for half an hour when James began to look concerned. Kate turned her head to see what was different about the car behind. Two men, Chinese-looking to her eye.

"Are they the men who were following you from Hong Kong?" asked Don. "And on the rubber plantation?"

"I can't tell. They've been tailing us for a few miles already."

James continued to drive steadily, the other car twenty yards behind.

"How fast can this car go?" asked Kate. "Could we give him the slip?"

"I'm glad you're not driving," said Emma with relief.

It must have gone on for half an hour but eventually, as the road widened, the following car accelerated and drew alongside, the girls instinctively trying to look small and clutching their bags close, though not consciously expecting gunfire. The Chinese driver gave them a friendly wave as he passed, seconded by a wave from his passenger.

"What are we doing with the treasure tonight?" asked Don. "If you put valuables in a hotel safe, criminals will know where to look. There may be a bank with a strong room but that still means alerting people to the worth of the deposit."

"We'll have to keep it close to us tonight," said James. "It's as well we don't have to go back tomorrow; we'd have had to hide half of it while fetching the rest."

Kate busied herself picturing possible hiding-places; Ophelia, who still had Aznavour in her head, was thinking of Madame Sir making a new life in retirement.

They arrived without the driver getting cramp, although his passengers were stiff with lack of leg-room, and no-one, as far as they could see, was hanging about waiting to rob them. Nevertheless, Don escorted the girls inside while James and Emma stayed together by the car, then Kate went back for another bag, returning with Emma, and Don went out again to join James in carrying the jade and the heaviest of the other bags.

"This should pay for a couple of volumes of Marco Polo," declared Don.

"If we can get it out of Thailand," said James with a worried look. "I don't know what the laws of treasure trove are in Thailand."

"Treasure trove has gone in England," remarked Emma.

"One of those silly changes," commented Don. "Reading the Riot Act is no more, so they don't know what to do when there's a riot."

"Emma, don't you have an ankle-length dress?" asked Kate.

"One with me. Why?"

"You could put it in a wardrobe with bags behind."

"Sound reasoning," approved Don.

"Are we going to divide them so that they're not all in one room?" asked Ophelia.

"That would be as well," said James. "I'll take a bag to my room. Before I go, I'd like you to choose something as a keepsake. You've been welcoming in Kuala Lumpur and helpful here. And I must give Dewey something; she wasn't happy with my using her library. I think I offended her."

"And Hazel," reminded Emma. "She wasn't invited."

"And she's a seasoned traveller," added Don. "We could have done with Dewey. She watches her library books like a hawk and she's quite belligerent at need."

"What are your plans, James?" asked Emma. "Cash could be transferred from a bank here to a branch in Kuala Lumpur but, if you deposit jade and gemstones, you'll have to pick them up later. The sooner we're back in Kuala Lumpur the better. Richard can give you advice on storing and selling the treasure. You could safely take some of it to Australia."

"Have you considered posting it to yourself?" asked Don. "I doubt if the Thai postal service is reliable enough."

A birthday cake sent from Hemel Hempstead to Leeds was found by the Royal Mail on a Glasgow railway station.

"I only thought as far as this," admitted James, rueful at being the impractical scholar. "I'll put this away for now."

"Ophelia doesn't want to go through the airport," said Kate as soon as he had gone, "and I'm not keen on it."

"That's what I thought." Emma was understanding.

"It's so complicated explaining how we came by the treasure," said Don, "that it would be better if we did not pass through customs."

"So we're going to be smugglers?"

"You could say so. We need to come ashore on the Malaysian side of the border, then catch a train to Kuala Lumpur."

"Our passports won't have been stamped on the way out," objected Emma, "so officially we'll still be in Thailand."

"We could say it was an oversight – or we'd gone out in a boat and been driven ashore beyond the border."

"That's plausible."

"There was a film on television," recalled Kate, "in which an East German family escaped to the West in a balloon at night."

"You would think of that," said Ophelia.

"A balloon? At night? Near the sea?" Emma put her foot down. Anyone who had seen Buster Keaton carried across America would have taken warning.

"It would be reckless," agreed Don. "I'll talk to James about it. In the meantime, decide on the best places to hide the treasure."

"I've wrapped the bust in a jumper." said Kate.

"That's appropriate – I thought it was full-length."

"This was at the bottom of a bag. Is it a sage, a philosopher?"

Don looked at it sagely.

"I don't recognise him – and I've been out East so long. You'd better put it back in the jumper; it could be precious to a collector."

"I feel sad for Madame Sir," said Ophelia. "Do you think she has only stayed there waiting for someone to come when she would have liked to go to France years ago?"

"That may be so," said Emma. "In retirement, she can rediscover her homeland."

"I'll keep watch tonight," said Don. "I'll suggest to James that he do the same – he'll be excited anyway. You can sleep the sleep of the just. You'll need your energy the next few days. If you find something worth millions, Kate, it's a two jumper treasure."

He was quietly enjoying the trip and was even resigned to sitting up all night without his records for company.

"You'd better take turns," said Emma, "or you'll fall asleep, and you'll be good for nothing tomorrow." After he had gone, Emma continued to supervise the hiding of hessian bags.

100

"Did James say we could choose whatever we like?" asked Kate.

"So long as it's not too valuable. Think it over. Choose something that will give you lasting pleasure and be a reminder of the adventure. We'd better spread these out, put some under hats, perhaps in shoes, under coats."

"Don hasn't taken anything to his room."

"He hasn't as much space and he may think that a man's clothes won't hide them as well."

"When are you expecting Mocha Joe?" asked Kate. "He knows where we went today."

"Not exactly."

"He has a good idea."

Up at the crack of dawn, Emma was sipping coffee, revitalising herself for the problems ahead.

"Did I hear talking?" asked Ophelia. "Whenever I woke up, I thought I could hear it."

"You did," confirmed Emma. "I recognised Don's voice, so I knew all must be well. They were on the verandah for us to be able to hear them. I couldn't make out what the conversation was about. Music or Marco Polo, I'd guess. Or sport. Men can talk for hours about sport."

"It's exciting, like waking on Christmas morning," said Ophelia. "I'd have liked to find jewels in a pillow-case at the foot of my bed."

"Did you wear the paintings under your pyjamas?"

"No. I left them in my trousers overnight."

"Such ingenuity."

"Are you up?" asked Don through the door.

"Just," answered Emma in a deceptively wide-awake tone. "You've been up all night. Come in and have a cup of coffee. We can't have you collapsing on us."

Don looked as well as might be expected.

"You can't stay up night after night," said Emma solicitously. "You're in need of a holiday in Kuala Lumpur."

"So am I," said Kate, emerging from her room. "And I'm supposed to be on holiday. After breakfast, could we say good-bye to the beach as we'll be leaving so soon?"

Emma looked at Don uncertainly, sorting out her thoughts as she spoke.

"If they're on the beach, they'll look like normal holidaymakers – which we are – so we should not attract attention."

"I think you're right. It will look odd if they're cooped up here for long."

So they had Don's blessing as well as Emma's. After breakfast, the girls were soon ready in bikinis and towels, only pausing for a quick look at the treasure.

Chapter Eight

Goodbye To The Beach

"I think I'd like a peridot," decided Ophelia. "Perhaps I'll be able to hear the music of the spheres."

"That's fanciful," said Kate.

"If I can't, it will be a happy reminder of them."

"Two would make ear-rings."

"James did not say we could have two and I like those I bought in Bangkok. I haven't worn them yet."

"I'd like a pearl," said Kate, "a white pearl set in a necklace of semi-precious stones: black agate, carnelian, jet, onyx, darker tones, with a pearl as the pièce de résistance."

The talk of gemstones had made Emma finger her pendant, proud that it could stand comparison so well.

"Amber is so rich in associations," said Emma. "The Ancients explained it as a piece of the sun come down to earth. It is said to be calming and to help you find a kindred spirit. I like all its colours but this is my favourite, the sunniest. I've seen moss green with cream inclusions, air bubbles or bits of leaf. Orange is the most common, there's a deep red and the rarest is milky." Hers was yellow. "I'm an amber person, soft and warm."

"How soft is it?"

"Much softer than diamond. You're not cracking it to find out."

Their change bikinis were hardly second best. Kate had red Santa hats on hers, Ophelia butterflies.

"You're not going to swim today?" Kate tried to persuade her cousin to change her mind.

"No. I'm too busy."

"You'll see George tomorrow." Emma smiled at that.

"I'll come with you as far as the shop," said Don, "to look around, just in case there are suspicious characters."

They were nearing the shop when a familiar figure came in to view from its landward side.

"What are you doing here, Andy? I thought you had business in Bangkok and points north."

"I have to chair a meeting between Thais and European businessmen. It requires finesse to make the most of commercial opportunities here. You have to know the customs and the character of individuals who are influential. No bribes, I hope, but judicious buttering up. I've learned a few things about it."

"They just happen to be meeting in a holiday resort."

"Why not? Business and pleasure. How did you get on with your treasure-seeking? Did you find anything?"

"Yes. More than I expected; more than James expected. We could do with bypassing customs to avoid complications, having to explain to officials that we came by them legitimately. They might be impounded for a time and some would go missing."

"I might be able to help."

"We'll be on the beach," cried Kate, breaking in to a jog, although it was already warm. They had to make the most of the beach before filing it in their memory with other beaches they had known.

They ran in to the water but did not stay long, feeling both restless and tired, more in a mood to doze on the beach than splash about.

"I'm tired," said Kate, "but I'm in a mood to dance. It must be my wild side."

"You have a tame side?"

"Soaking up sea and sunshine, exploring the fish's element. When I see a beach like this, I can't wait to sample the water – but after a while I prefer the sand."

"You can dance the night away but you can't swim the night away," said Ophelia.

"I never dance all night," said Kate.

"But you like to dance longer than you like to swim."

"That's true. I enjoy going for a swim but I enjoy lying in the sun watching people and letting them watch me – you like that. How long do Australian surfers spend in the water?" She might well ask. Are Australian beach babes Water Babies?

"I don't think I've known a better beach," went on Ophelia, looking around the bay, "but I've seen more interesting countries."

Her sister paused to think about it, then nodded. Lightly toasted, Kate felt she was glowing with vitality.

"Don't let yourself be burnt on your last day."

Kate gave herself up to her sister's ministrations, then turned the cream on her. Although there were more people on the beach, they had been able to leave their towels unattended.

"Are there holiday beaches in Malaysia?" asked Ophelia.

"Probably. But it is a Moslem country. The sight of you in a bikini might excite men," teased Kate. "You haven't brought your sketch-book. I thought what interested you was people and places associated with people."

"No-one's taken my fancy."

Beach on beach, so many beaches in a drowsy head, remembering one while lying on another, white sand, yellow sand trickling in an hourglass; once the hourglass shape was in vogue...in late nineteenth century Europe?

"Did I hear?" mused Kate, "that Captain Cook's men found peridots at the bottom of the sea in Tahiti and thought they were green diamonds?"

"Can't be true. It would have been mentioned more often. They could have made their fortunes like that. Peridots do get about though."

Half-heartedly, Kate sat up, regarding the sea, the boldest bathers some way out, others, more numerous, in the shallows, her sun-creamed arm as she stretched a reminder of the inconvenience of going in to the water again...and putting cream on again, which would be work for Ophelia.

"Heidelberg I like." Ophelia's words turned Kate away from the sea.

"I do. And I like Kuala Lumpur. I'll be glad to get back and see more of it."

"I hope we do leave by sea. Does Andy grow on you?"

"Maybe." Kate was noncommittal. "He did help us," she reminded herself.

"I feel guilty," said Ophelia, "lazing on the beach when Emma is guarding the treasure and worrying about how to get it to Kuala Lumpur."

"I feel guilty about nearly being killed."

"George will be back before we leave, won't he?"

"He's bound to be."

"Will George travel back separately – if he is returning to Kuala Lumpur?"

"I hope he is. We can't bring them together if they're apart, thousands of miles apart. He seems worthy of Emma."

"You're not going to find her someone better? Shall we go in once more, then straight back to the hotel?"

"Yes. A quick plunge and out. We have important things to do."

She drew herself up to her full height, then checked that her briefs weren't slipping.

"Do you particularly want a swim?" asked Ophelia.

"You've changed your mind quickly. That's not like you."

"We've been on the look-out for Chinese," recalled Ophelia. "There they are. You'd think they were trying to look like Hong Kong gangsters in a film. How can they be holidaymakers?"

"How long have they been looking at us?"

"They're not. They're studiously not looking at us. Are they waiting to see if James comes along – or Don – probably James."

Kate knew that her sister's eye would detect whether people were pretending not to look at them.

"There ought to have been more boys looking at us," occurred to her.

"They're admiring you discreetly," explained Ophelia. "But those... three men are not discreet; they're suspicious."

"You weren't sure there were three. Has one gone away?"

"I don't think so. They were here when we came out of the sea and they're not doing anything; they're not sunbathing."

"We'd better go and tell the others," said Kate.

"Mm." The observers were on Ophelia's mind. "Where do you think Jim is? Looking out for us or watching someone else?"

"We'll probably find out. Don't look at them," said Kate. They reached the shop and looked in the windows, which gave them a chance to turn and glance where the men had been apparently by accident.

"They're not on the beach," said Kate, "and they're not following us openly. Where have they gone?"

She liked to know who was tailing her at what distance. As they approached the hotel, she glanced over her shoulder several times.

"You told me not to look," reminded Ophelia. Caught out disregarding her own counsel, Kate kept silent. To their surprise, Emma was alone but before they could change Don arrived.

"Have you been talking to James?" asked Emma.

"No. Andy."

"Where did you go with him?" asked Kate.

"To see one of his acquaintances. Andy said he could get us a boat."

"Mocha Joe has already offered me one," said Emma.

"He likes you," said Kate.

"He likes you."

"Did he go in to detail?" asked Don.

"No. It doesn't seem to be his way."

"Andy knows someone with a yacht. I'd expect it to be conspicuous."

"With a motor?"

"Oh, yes. We'd not be dependent on sail. I'm not sure how much of a sailor Andy is."

"Did Andy offer you a choice of sizes?"

"Not yet."

"We have an embarrassment of boats."

"If we're smuggling," said Kate, "we should go with the smuggler."

Emma was trying to weigh up the possible courses of action.

"We have the impression that Andy's a sailor. Is he?"

"He thinks he's a sailor. Confidence can go a long way."

"Do you have confidence in Andy?" asked Ophelia.

"No."

"Mocha Joe?"

"No. I don't think they'll sink us but they may set us ashore in the wrong place."

"Have you consulted James?" asked Emma.

"No. I thought you might have spoken to him. Where is he?"

Kate looked at her sister. It was time to mention the Chinese.

"You remember that James thought he was being followed?"

"Yes. From Hong Kong." Emma was beginning to look worried. "What have you seen?"

"Chinese. On the beach. They seemed to be watching us but they're probably the same men who kept close to James on the plane from Hong Kong and in the rubber plantation."

"We hoped they might have bigger fish to fry," recalled Don.

"I haven't seen him or heard him this morning. Has he been having a nap?" asked Emma. "You were talking much of the night."

"I'll just check his room," said Don; in the meantime the girls washed the suncream off and changed.

"He hasn't taken the bag of jade," said Don, returning, "and he hasn't packed his pyjamas. He's expecting to come back here tonight. If he'd been snatched from his room, you would have heard something – I think."

"They would have come here for the rest of the treasure."

"Might George come with us?" asked Kate. "He may know a bit about boats."

"I don't know," repied Emma, who might have been expected to know if anyone did. "He may be busy and I haven't heard him talk about boats."

"If we pass the border in darkness," said Don, "the customs will be looking out for contraband; if we pass in daylight, we'll be day trippers gone astray."

"That's what Mocha Joe said."

"I'm on my way to becoming a smuggler."

"Is he going to come with us?" asked Kate. "Mocha Joe, I mean."

"He did not say so but he may do."

"Does James trust him?"

"Who knows whom James trusts? In any case James doesn't know him."

"You don't know him very well," pointed out Emma. "Nor do I."

There was a sound of footsteps on the verandah, heralding the scholar's arrival; which was a relief. He had not been kidnapped.

"Where have you been, James?"

"Checking timetables for the flight to Bangkok." Don looked at Emma.

"We're planning to go by boat to avoid awkwardness going through the customs."

"Is that necessary?"

"It's advisable."

"You remember that you were being followed," recalled Kate, "or thought you were. We've seen Chinese on the beach, who were watching us, probably because we're with you."

"Are you sure of that? I haven't seen them here." In sight of success, he had forgotten his anxiety.

"They could be watching you from a distance," said Emma, "because they don't know we have the treasure."

"I may have been imagining it." He was determined to be upbeat now.

"I still think we should be wary," insisted Emma.

"I'm ahead of myself with the book," said James, "imagining what I'll find in my coming research, sketching it in, drawing provisional conclusions. Another year and I'll know whether I'm on to something."

"Have you lived with Marco Polo long?" asked Ophelia.

"Since childhood. I decided to write a book about him some years ago. It looked as though funding would dry up."

"He seems dull to me," said Don. "The man, that is, not the places he visited."

Don was appreciative of his work without being able to share his enthusiasm.

After James had gone, he said to the others:

"If I discovered something about Marco Polo, it would give me satisfaction but I'd rather write a beautiful melody."

"I would," said Ophelia, "and I'm not a musician."

"When will Andy get in touch with us?" asked Emma.

"Very soon," answered Don. "He has to fit us in between his various meetings."

"You should volunteer to illustrate the book," suggested Kate to her sister, who was too diffident to act on the advice. "Talk to him while he's excited," she urged." Reluctantly, Ophelia did as she was told. "Have you got a commission?" asked Kate on her return.

"No. We talked about Marco Polo and the Mongols and Venetian art and the Doge diverting the fourth Crusade to Constantinople because the Byzantines had blinded him."

"You covered some ground," said Emma admiringly.

"But no commission?" Kate seemed to feel that a talent for drawing needed drive to make its mark. She would complement her sister, make good her lack of drive.

Don had been cogitating on their plans to leave Thailand. He went to hear if Alldridge had any thoughts on the matter but came straight back.

"We've lost James again."

"I think he's gone to return the hired car," informed Ophelia.

"So we're going to...by bus?" conjectured Emma.

"I think we can get a lift," said Don. "We could not have driven a hired car over the border nor could we have abandoned it."

"Are we still keeping telephone silence?" asked Emma, "and hiding from cyberspace or in cyberspace? I'm not sure which we're hiding from: Hong Kong gangsters or the C.I A.."

"Both," declared Kate expansively. "It's a dangerous world."

"You should know," retorted her cousin. "When you haven't had a narrow escape, I'll let your parents know that all is well. Better drowned than duffers – he would not have said: better stabbed than duffers."

"And we're going to sea," reminded Ophelia to put Emma's mind at rest. Andy breezed in while they were eating afternoon tea.

"I can have a boat ready within thirty-six hours. Would you rather be comfortable or inconspicuous?"

"I'd like to be both," said Don. "Are you offering us a taste of luxury? It's not the sort of yacht which is moored at the Cannes Film Festival, is it?"

"I'm afraid not. They seldom come so far afield-or-awater. It's comfortable though – you don't want to look like refugees, do you?"

"Not me. I'd rather pass for a millionaire."

"You said there was a choice." Kate jumped on the discrepancy.

"There's a fishing boat to fall back on."

"Falling back on fish," considered Emma. "I'd go with the other one."

"That's settled. It's not from the one you spoke to; it's more seaworthy, with a better motor. Your trip's worked out well; I didn't think much would come of it. I'd congratulate James if he were here."

"He keeps disappearing," said Don. "His inner Marco Polo has been activated. I'd rather he stayed with us in case he was right about gangsters dogging his steps."

This may have reminded Andy as he was leaving:

"By the way, I've just heard of a shooting on the road from Bangkok. Bernstein's car was ambushed..."

"By Red Shirts?"

"No. I don't think there are any here. It appears to have been attacked by robbers but there may be a political motive. Dangerous business, intelligence or special forces, particularly if you make enemies as he did."

But when Andy reported to them only half an hour later they learned that the driver had been found dead, with his wallet in his pocket.

"Shot," said Andy. "The car had careered off the road; the petrol tank was nearly empty, otherwise the whole vehicle might have gone up in flames. Bernstein's number-plate was on it but the car wasn't the one I last saw him driving. The wallet and passport settled it.

Bernstein wasn't driving the car; George Berson was."

Ophelia moved to support Emma, then Don took over, his arm across her back above Ophelia's.

"Who switched the number-plate?" he asked. "Not George."

"Only Bernstein has a motive," said Andy. "He was using George as a decoy. The police have reacted slowly. I asked if you could identify the body in situ to get it over with. A morgue is so impersonal and you'd have to travel farther. I'm afraid I have to leave now to talk to some businessmen, then I have a meeting at an ungodly hour in the morning, selling British universities."

"George said he was going to give Bangkok twenty-four hours," recalled Emma. "He could not have set out so soon. Could he?" Emma pleaded with fate.

"I think you'd better lie down," said Don, taking her arm with his other hand. He led her to her bed, the girls following, at a loss until:

"Would you like a cup of tea?" asked Kate, finding something useful to do. "Yes, please." Kate sped to perform her task.

"These are the directions," said Andy. "I think I only met him once, so it would be better if you identified him."

Hardly had he gone than another visitor arrived. Mocha Joe must have been waiting for Andy to leave, wary of someone who associated with officials. He looked surprised not to be received by Emma.

"You've met George," said Kate. He nodded. "Andy Ashdown thinks he may have been killed, shot driving from Bangkok. Someone should identify him. Andy has rushed off to one of his meetings and can't be back for hours. I think, we think that Emma should know the worst or be relieved."

"I liked him," said Mocha Joe. "How did it happen?"

"Andy said they thought they had killed Bernstein. He must have switched the number-plates, using George as a decoy."

"His fellow-countryman." It flashed through Kate's mind: who were Mocha Joe's fellow-countrymen? "It wasn't by chance then. Was he hoping to go in to hiding after faking his own death?"

"Andy said there wasn't much petrol in the tank, otherwise the car would have burst in to flames."

"So there would have been no means of identification."

Hearing that there was another visitor, Emma came from her room. Mocha Joe's eyes met Don's in a less guarded way than at their first meeting.

"Do you know where it happened?"

Don held out the sheet of paper on which Andy had written directions.

"I can take you there," said Mocha Joe. "You'll find out for sure whether he is dead. The police will move the body before long."

"He'd come a long way," said Emma. "I thought it had happened near Bangkok."

"He was hurrying here to see you." Kate's voice faltered as she met her sister's eyes. Would her words make Emma feel better or worse for knowing that George had been eager to see her?

"I've found you a boat," said Mocha Joe. "It's moored not far from the border. You'll be sneaking around customs and passport control, not making a long sea voyage. I forgot you had a car. I'll still take you; I know the road better than James."

"He's taken the car back," informed Kate.

"I'd better take you then."

"Do you know Andy?" asked Emma.

"I know of him."

"More of Bernstein?"

"Yes." He sighed in sympathy with her bitterness.

"Andy has arranged to borrow someone's yacht. We're grateful to you." Ophelia detected disappointment in his face at the mention of Andy's boat. "It won't be flashy," he argued, "but it may be more suitable, fading in to the background."

"Which is what you like to do." He smiled at her insight.

"We could look at both boats before deciding."

"How much would it cost?" asked Don, recalled from tragedy to finance.

"No more than a hired car." Don smiled approvingly at his willingness to forgo a commission.

"There's James," said Kate as she heard him returning. Don was off the horns of a dilemma. He had been vexed at needing to watch over the treasure when his duty was to go with Emma. Seeing her face, Alldridge looked perplexed.

"We think her friend has been killed," explained Mocha Joe in an undertone.

"In a car-crash?"

"Shot, driving. Emma..." He glanced at her, "or Don will identify the body."

"Should I go and hire the car again?" asked James.

"No," answered Don. "It would take too long and we have transport."

James looked helplessly at Emma, then her cousins for inspiration.

"You ought to stay here to hold the fort, James," reminded Don. "Those Chinese could be about."

"You girls need not come," Emma forced herself to say.

"But we do need to come," contradicted Kate. "Don't we, Don?"

"Yes," he agreed. "You'd better."

"Jim will stand guard," said Mocha Joe. "If he checks that you're all right, don't be alarmed; he's not Chinese. I'll go and tell him what has happened. I'll be back by the time you're ready."

James was at a loss, jolted from planning his book by the suspected tragedy. He sat down, got up, drifted towards the door as if to go back to his own room, and came back.

"I'm beginning to visualise the various sections," he said, more at ease in his book. "It's a help knowing I'll have the wherewithal to finish."

A bit of a scholar manqué, Don warmed to his enthusiasm.

"You'll be inspired now."

"Can you picture the cover as well?" asked Ophelia. "The right one would give it more impact." Kate thought of suggesting her sister to design the cover but it seemed the wrong time.

"You could invite Jim for a cup of tea," suggested Emma, trying to be hospitable. "He's partial to Keemun China. There are some biscuits here."

They went outside at the sound of a car.

"We can put our trust in James and Jim," reassured Don. "Do you think Jim would like to hear about Marco Polo?"

"You never know."

Emma welcomed the joke with a weak smile.

Kate was in the back seat this time, remembering her first drive in the car when it was early evening; this time it was soon dark. Mocha Joe was silent for a few minutes before saying:

"The sooner you leave here the better. There are Hong Kong gangsters interested in what you've found. They've had their sights elsewhere the past few days but they'll soon come back to James and his quest. They heard about it before I did. If they think you've found something, they may exaggerate its value."

"How dangerous are they?"

"I only know them from a distance, by hearsay, but I think they've committed murder in the underworld, not so far outside it."

"Thanks for warning us," said Don.

It was not a long journey. Kate's fingers tapped the rhythm of a tune, consciously slowing and almost stopping the tapping, her cousin's thoughts, she feared, racing.

Mocha Joe had put the directions aside and was looking out for the scene of the shooting.

"We're nearly there." Sure enough, they saw a knot of people ahead, some uniformed, around a wrecked car at the side of the road. Parking ten yards away, the smuggler left Don to present his credentials. The conversation with police and a man from the coroner's office tried the patience of those watching from the car but eventually Don came back to open the door for Emma. They approached the scene. Kate was on that side of the car, trying to make out what she could of the wreck through gaps in the bystanders. Were Don and Emma deliberately trying to obscure her view? Surely, they had other things to think about.

"I have a flask of coffee," said Mocha Joe, "and a drop of brandy. I suppose your cousin drinks it even less than I do."

115

"Normally," said Ophelia, "but this isn't normal."

"Would you like coffee without the brandy?"

"Yes, please." He poured coffee in to a cup and handed it to her.

"They're talking to the same men," complained Kate. "What's going on?"

"Formalities," said Ophelia, as though experienced in dealing with bureaucrats. She sipped her coffee approvingly, leaning closer to Kate and forward, trying to get a different angle.

"They're going closer now," said Mocha Joe. And the bystanders seemed to melt away, leaving the three in the car a clear view of Don and Emma and beyond them the wreck.

Chapter Nine

Amber

George lay half-in, half-out of his car as though he had tried to rise and walk away but slumped as he did so.

"Shall I identify him?" asked Don grimly.

"I knew him better," insisted Emma.

"We'll do it together."

So Emma's mind revolved memories of scenes with George, interspersed with George's bloody corpse, far off, then jolted by the present, yet unaware that Don was holding her up. Kate gripped the handle of the car door.

"Wait," said Mocha Joe. Being Kate, she persisted in opening the door a few inches, met his eyes in the mirror, closed the door, her tears beginning to run. As Ophelia hugged her sister, the thought crossed her mind: how many violent deaths has Mocha Joe witnessed or nearly witnessed? Has anyone dear to him been murdered?

Don helped Emma to the car, Kate got out to make way for her, then she sat down between the girls. Don went back to sign a statement that the deceased was George Berson.

"Mocha Joe has some brandy," Ophelia told Emma. "Not neat; in coffee."

"Brandy," repeated Emma, looking at Don for advice as he got in to the car. "A drop might revive you; a generous dram would do more harm than good." The coffee was poured out, brandy measured carefully.

"Only a drop please." She wet her lips with the brandy as though making her last drop of water last as long as possible in a desert.

Ophelia was feeling whether her wrist was cold or feverish, wondering which was more alarming. Cold. Going colder. She hugged her cousin more tightly.

"Are you ready?" asked Don.

"Yes." She still did not cry effusively. A tear ran down her cheek and another. A fierce mood crossed Mocha Joe's face, then he concentrated on the road. Like the woman interviewer who professed to be frightened by Yves Montand's passionate denunciation of communism, Ophelia was disturbed by the anger that showed fleetingly in Mocha Joe's face. On reflection, she was glad he was angry; that was what anger was for. Trying to hug the hurt out of their cousin, they only spoke in the hope of diverting her attention.

At length she said: "I should send a card of condolence to his family but I don't know their address."

"Could an American consulate find out quickly? They could be given the number of his passport. Dewey and Hazel would probably like to sign it. If you send a card when we're back in Kuala Lumpur, it won't be too late."

Assenting to Don's suggestion with a weary nod, Emma could look forward to choosing her card.

"Should we sign it too?" asked Ophelia, "or send a separate one?"

"Sign the same one. You're with me."

"Will George be buried in America?" asked Kate.

"Yes. I don't know whether a member of his family will come out to Bangkok or wait at the airport."

The rest of the drive back was in silence, the girls' eyes from time to time meeting the reflections of their cousin's, of Don's, of Mocha Joe's.

"We're very grateful," said Don as they approached the hotel. "I hope you have better luck here than George. If you are familiar with Thailand, the authorities must be getting to know you."

"Thank you for your concern. You may be right."

"Will you be coming with us?" asked Kate.

"Andy's better at talking his way past officials. He's respectable."

"Would you like to be?" He smiled.

"I'll drive you down the coast; we should set off by late afternoon – if you're all well enough. Emma's likely to feel better at home among friends."

"Why are you helping us?"

"I seldom meet people like you in this line of work. Oh, I forgot James," he recalled. "I doubt if there's room in the car for one more – not for a long journey."

"And you forgot Jim. Does he appear magically?" asked Kate. "How does he get about?"

"If Andy's going with you in the boat, he'll need to drive down and meet you soon after dawn tomorrow. He could take James."

"And Jim."

"Mm."

"Are you wary of Jim talking to Andy and giving too much away?" His smile acknowledged her perception. "Andy moves in different circles. Would you expect Jim to give much away?"

"No. Unless he's giving directions to a tattooist."

James had heard the car and come out, accompanied, they noticed, by Jim. He could tell by Emma's face there had been no mistake.

"My sympathy."

"Thank you."

"I'm glad to see you hit it off," said Don as Jim waved goodbye to the scholar and joined Mocha Joe in the car.

"It's surprising how many people think about Marco Polo from time to time." His readership might be bigger than he had feared.

Still looking dazed, Emma made her way indoors as quickly as her unsteady steps could take her, Kate in close attendance lest she feel faint.

"You'd better lie down," said Kate. "Do you feel like a light fish dish or just fruit?"

"Neither until I've had a rest."

"You don't want sleeping pills." Don was telling her, not asking her. "I haven't brought any of my records; they might have helped."

They tucked her up in bed, then went out on to the verandah to talk to Don.

"We'll be nearby," promised Kate, "and we'll keep looking in to be sure you are well."

Ophelia whispered to her sister.

"He would have been in Thailand anyway," pointed out Kate. "You said he planned to come here before he heard about our trip."

Kate waited to be sure her cousin had registered that.

"James has gone to his room," said Don. "He doesn't know what he can do to help; there' s always his book to work on."

"I hope he doesn't feel left out," said Ophelia, "That he's only one of us when we're treasure seeking." Don was thinking about something else.

"Did George give her that amber pendant?"

"No. But he was a piece of the sun for her."

"And you are," reminded Don. "Looking after you and making you happy will take her mind off her grief."

"So it's our duty to be happy?"

"I think so, Kate."

The three of them were silent for a time, sufficiently at ease not to need to speak, the girls hoping not to hear Emma crying, Don for all they knew casting his mind back to past sorrows.

Kate stood up: "I'll see how she is." To Ophelia's inquiring look she murmured: "You come next time."

Kate found her cousin studying a black blouse, shaking her head at a black skirt – "I can't wear that – inappropriate." spreading out a scarf, which contained black but also bright colours.

"Jet," suggested Kate. "Would black pearls be too showy?"

"It's not a wedding. I haven't any jet; it doesn't appeal to me."

"You will keep wearing amber? George would have liked you to. And yellow will go well with black; there's no reason why you should not be elegant when in mourning." Kate almost bit her lip, then decided her tone was right.

"I'll wear amber. It may have helped me find a soulmate; perhaps it will help me find another someday."

"Is it the first time you've called George your soulmate?"

"I don't know if he was. I needed much more time to be sure.

I don't want to make a display. I'm not a member of his family; I wasn't engaged to him; it should be the low-key acknowledgement of a friend."

Kate could tell by the word acknowledgement that Emma was composed, thinking clearly, but Kate could also detect the pain just below the surface. Thinking and talking about clothes can restore a woman's equilibrium if not her equanimity. Kate sorted through her cousin's clothes, holding up a black cashmere jumper.

"Warm," said Emma. "I don't know why I brought it. I wear more white than black."

"Ophelia wants to know how you are. Shall I tell her to come in?"

"Yes."

Ophelia was on her feet the instant she saw her sister, registering the degree of anxiety in Kate's face. "We need you to help Emma decide what to wear in mourning." Ophelia hurried to add her ideas while Don, intrigued by feminine preoccupations, weighed up what this said about Emma's state of mind.

"I remember what he said to me before leaving Kuala Lumpur: "You must come to New England some day."

"Go to New England. You haven't been there for a long time."

"Do you think he belonged there?" asked Kate. "He had itchy feet. Where does a rolling stone settle? On the slopes of a volcano, so life will never be dull?"

"He liked warm water swimming yet he liked Bhutan," recalled Ophelia.

"You don't think he had a girl in every port or every stopping-off place?"

Ophelia frowned at Kate's being tactless. Emma took no offence.

"I don't think of George in New England. I think of him mainly in Kuala Lumpur – and here. I did think that seeing the place where he grew up would have helped me get to know him better but now I'm not so sure."

"Did he show you photographs of his home and family?"

"Sparingly. He did show me many photographs he had taken on his travels. He must have thought they were closer to his present self.

He talked about his travels much more than his studies."

"Did he ever say what he was looking for?"

"Not me. Marriage was a few countries down the line. I'll lock George away in my bottom drawer." Emma was thinking herself out of the belief that she had almost been a fiancée.

"That black and grey scarf," picked out Ophelia. "It's unobtrusively pretty; not eye-catching perhaps but you don't want that. I think it would grow on you and anyone looking at it. Why haven't I seen you wearing it?"

"You haven't been here many days. You can't expect a fashion parade."

Emma held up several garments for inspection before deciding on the scarf. "Will you start wearing it when we get back to Malaysia? It might be splashed with seawater."

"I suppose I'd better do that."

"It's something pretty to wear in memory of George."

There was a knock at the door and they heard Don talking to a visitor.

"Jim's voice?" queried Kate. She went out to check. Jim had brought a message from Mocha Joe, with a map of the best jumping-off point and the coast either side of the border.

"I'm sorry about George," said Jim. "I hope your friend is well."

"On the mend," assured Emma defiantly from the doorway. "Would you like some Keemun China before you go?"

He considered his commitments for a few moments, then nodded: "Yes. I'd enjoy that."

"It's my travelling tea," said Emma. "My favourite is Darjeeling – and Luaka Ceylon I like."

Playing the hostess must have been too much for her at such a stressful time, for she looked tired already as she poured out tea, Kate standing by to grab the pot, Jim seemingly aware that she was.

"I hope you'll feel better when you get home," and he left to carry out whatever mission was next on his list.

Meanwhile Emma subsided in to an arm-chair. Did the proximity of her cousins make it easier to give way to sleep? As soon as Jim had left, Don had gone out to do some packing, complicated by the need to hide gems and a figurine. Ready to leave, he hurried back. A cushion had been placed behind Emma's head.

"Has she been asleep?" asked Don.

"Yes. For half an hour."

"That will do her good. I forgot to ask: do you suffer from sea-sickness?".

"Not as far as we know but we've never been on particularly choppy seas."

Another knock, louder this time, was accompanied by Andy opening the unlocked door and striding in. Was it his gait for action rather than conferences?

"It was George," confirmed Don, trying not to wake Emma.

"I'll soon have you out of here," promised Andy.

"Would you mind if we didn't take your boat? You would not feel slighted?"

"Not at all, but what alternative arrangements have you made?"

"They include you. We'd like you to take us in the boat Mocha Joe has provided; it may be less conspicuous than yours, being supplied by smugglers."

"Does it have a false bottom? Is it known to the police?"

"He wouldn't do that," protested Kate.

"How did your recruiting go?" asked Don. "Do they pay you a commission?"

"Not exactly. I've recruited seven or eight – one was doubtful. They've heard about Menezes being shot on the Tube. I put their minds at rest. I said it was a one-off; the Metropolitan Police don't make a habit of killing foreigners."

"It wouldn't put my mind at rest," murmured Ophelia.

"Jim brought a map," said Don, holding it out. "Is that a good place to embark?" Andy studied it, no doubt calculating distances.

"That's as good a place as any along the coast. Our aim is to make land beyond the border by dusk. We don't want to be at sea in the dark."

"We certainly don't," agreed Kate.

"There isn't room for us all in one car," continued Don. "Could you bring James with you? When can you start out?"

"No problem. I can take him to dinner with some academics. A couple of them study East Asian history. He could find the conversation interesting, even do a bit of networking. If you're driving overnight to be there by dawn, we can meet you soon afterwards."

"That's better than I expected," said Don. "I had visions of James being left alone here and being robbed. Some things are beginning to work out."

"That's settled then. I'll pick James up in half an hour."

"To go where?" asked Alldridge, opening the door. He had recognized Andy's voice and come to find out what was being planned.

"How would you like to meet some Thai scholars?" asked Andy. "Not all Thais. One's Chinese and another's here from Australia for a term. There are specialists in East Asian history – you never know what you might pick up – and I can promise you a good dinner. We'll then drive south overnight and rendezvous with the others soon after dawn. We ought really to synchronise watches."

"I bet Mocha Joe's never synchronised watches in his life," remarked Don.

"Not even with Jim?" Kate did not forget him.

"Half an hour," repeated James. "I'd better start packing. I do have stout leather bags which should keep my manuscripts dry."

"I'll do my best to bring you and your manuscripts safe to Kota Bahru."

"Is that where we're going?" asked Kate.

"Very near there."

James hastened away to pack the treasures of past artisans and the treasures of his research.

"It'll be like old times." Andy was in high spirits. "I'm looking forward to it."

"What larks, eh?" said Don to himself.

"What'll be like old times?" asked Emma sleepily. "Did I hear James?"

"You did. Andy's taking him out to dinner with academics. He could make some useful contacts, fill a gap in his research."

"James will want to feel he has done it all himself, not relied on patronage."

"That's true, Andy. Scholars are proud who don't belong to the establishment. Could you do his networking for him?"

"I thought we were – did someone say we were setting out this afternoon?"

Not yet fully awake, Emma tried to recall conversations she had heard or maybe dreamt. "It's all settled," declared Andy. "The matter's in hand."

"I'm glad we're going in Mocha Joe's boat," said Ophelia. "He offered to help and, if we'd turned him down, it might have hurt his feelings."

"You're imagining him sensitive for a smuggler," pointed out Emma.

"He may not always have been a smuggler. We don't know what else he may have been."

"Perhaps it's better not to inquire," suggested Don.

"I see he's marked the inlet where the boat is moored," noticed Andy. "We should be able to locate it easily enough."

"What about petrol?" asked Don. "You're here and Mocha Joe will be here soon. Who's at the boat now checking whether it has petrol?"

"It should be easy to buy some on the coast. I should think he will have arranged for the boat to be refuelled ready for a prompt start. He may have had something else in mind, delayed only by our trip."

"So we are going in late afternoon?" A drowsy Emma sought clarification.

"Yes. In three days' time you'll be home and see Dewey and Hazel."

But not George. Was Andy chary of mentioning George? He tacitly assumed that Emma was out of sorts but without mentioning the reason.

"I'll go and finalise arrangements for the dinner," continued Andy. "They'll put James's name in his place and I'll see that there's someone near him he can talk to. They'll all know some English but he'll want to be among historians." Andy hesitated at the door, glancing at Emma: "All the best."

"I'd better start getting ready," she decided, slowly, sleepily rising. "When we're back home in Kuala Lumpur, I'll luxuriate in a bath with fragrant oils for hours on end. Cold showers may revive but they're not the same."

She did have a bar of mild, agreeable soap made by people who think human beings' eyes are more important than lip service to animal rights.

"I'll order some food," said Don, "and tell them we're leaving and we'll be back to pay by mid-afternoon."

"We'd better ask for a packed lunch," asked Kate, filling in for Emma. "It's going to be a long journey tonight and tomorrow."

"You're not confident of catching fish?" joked Don.

"We'd have nowhere to cook it. The boat will have a tiny galley if there is one. I'll come with you to help carry the food. Will you be all right, Ophelia? James is near and Emma will be out of the shower soon."

Ophelia first nodded, then said: "Yes" pensively. Whatever was on her mind Kate would inquire about when they came back. On the verandah, in an undertone, Kate remarked: "Andy didn't say much to Emma." "No. He didn't," agreed Don. "He won't have known what to say."

They had been gone a few minutes when Emma's head peeped around the door, followed by the rest of Emma, wrapped in a towel.

"No strange men," reassured Ophelia. "Do you like Thailand?" she suddenly asked. "There is an undercurrent of violence here and it could get worse."

"Will get worse, I expect. Kuala Lumpur's more relaxed. I don't think I'm biased because it was a British colony; Malaysia's better run than Thailand; Japan must be more efficient than either but Tokyo's notoriously overcrowded. Don and Dewey told me about Chinese being massacred in Indonesia in the nineteen sixties; there haven't been massacres in Malaysia. Is that the influence of the British Empire? It has done more good than the B.B.C. ever admits."

George would have enjoyed seeng Emma in a bath-towel, thought Ophelia. She must divert her cousin's thoughts to..."How should I wear a peridot?" Emma found solace in Ophelia's face.

"Near enough to your eyes but not too close, blue and green together. Did I see you with blue earrings you haven't worn? Blue and blue and green." As comforting as a Vermeer painting.

Footsteps made Emma hurriedly adjust her towel. Still drowsy, she took a step towards the bathroom as Kate pushed open the door and entered followed by Don. Emma relaxed. "Only Don," to Ophelia; "You've always liked Dorothy Lamour," to Don. "I do but mainly for the songs."

"There'll be a stream of men coming through here," reminded Kate, taking charge and restoring propriety, which was novel for Kate. Emma dutifully went to dress. Don smiled at the incongruity.

"Dressing down the schoolmistress for not being dressed," he whispered when Emma was no longer within hearing. He had no wish to discomfort her. "Were you afraid that Emma would marry Andy?" asked Ophelia.

"I'd not have been happy about it. I don't think he would have suited her. George might have been a better match but where would he have taken her?"

"Emma's ears will pick up your whispering," said Kate, "and she'll wonder what's going on."

"Emma was talking about massacres in Indonesia but not Malaysia because of the British influence. Weren't there massacres in India in 1947?"

"Yes. Horrific. A million people were killed. The British tried to keep the lid on it until Lord Mountbatten withdrew in a hurry. He claimed there was nothing he could do, others thought he could have alleviated the suffering. The Indian sub-continent is so big, with a long history of religious conflict. After Indira Gandhi was shot by her Sikh bodyguards, nearly three thousand Sikhs were massacred by mobs led by Congress politicians while Hindu policemen stood by doing nothing. Rajiv Gandhi waited three days before telling the army to restore order. The Indian subcontinent has only ever been united for a century under British rule."

"Is the north-west the most lawless part?" asked Kate.

"I'm not sure. A journalist suggested that the British ought to have colonised the region properly but no-one ever has pacified it. India has traditionally been raided over the Hindu-Kush. But India itself is a violent place: in the past thirty years there have been massacres of Sikhs, Moslems and Christians, bloodshed in clashes between castes. Indian governments have found India an intractable problem as the British Empire did. The British did manage with a much smaller civil service. I was proud to hear an Indian say that he never knew of an Englishman take a bribe. That's the good side of imperialism."

"I'm glad there's a good side," said Emma, now dressed for the journey. She was waiting to put on mourning, taking in George's death thought by thought, dallying with imagination of her own death, of another Ice Age, of the sun going out. She looked buffeted rather than drawn.

"You girls had better get ready. We haven't much time."

Hardly had she spoken before Andy returned, his brisk bonhomie always making him appear slightly bigger than he was. A Norfolk jacket of apparent quality and numerous pockets was a concession to academe, as were the smart, creased trousers but his shirt was still open-necked; he apparently made a point of that. Kate's curiosity was drawn to hairy chests, even a hint of a hairy chest. Did Andy feel that being a bit of a Mountain Man made people trust him more at conferences, he was not dapper enough to be a banker?

"One of the perks of the job," he noted. "Sometimes I'm listening to boring people and all I get is tea and biscuits."

"Do academics dine well?" asked Kate.

"Not as well as university administrators."

"You enjoy it then? Most of it?"

"I miss action sometimes but this is varied – and I get about."

"Was England too tame for you?"

"Maybe. Was it too tame for Don? For you?" He did not mention Emma.

"You've found a niche all over South-East Asia," joked Don. "How far do you range, Andy? China? Japan?"

"I've been to both, helping to sell British goods. I'm nearly as well travelled as Hazel." They all recognised that she took the palm.

"Does she go to many places besides Kuala Lumpur?" asked Ophelia.

"She goes everywhere," said Andy. "The globe-trotter par excellence."

"But she still loves Kuala Lumpur?" Did Ophelia have George in mind?

"She certainly does," confirmed Don. "L.A.'s nothing to K.L. – Spain she finds acceptable. Has she been to New Zealand?"

"She was full of New Zealand," recalled Emma, easing her mind with thoughts of someone else's holiday. "She wasn't keen on Sydney."

"Too brash?"

"Probably. Some people think it's beautiful. Should we call James?"

"I'm here," said the scholar, lugging bags that seemed to have multiplied. Kate decided he must have had one bag folded in another when they arrived.

"I have settled up with you, Don, haven't I?" he checked.

"Yes," Don confirmed. "Enjoy the evening. You never know, you may find a subject for your next book." Andy wrested a bag from James's grasp, very likely one the scholar wanted to keep close to him.

"Will there be alcohol at the dinner?" asked Emma.

"I promise to go on the wagon until we're in the boat."

"We don't mind you having a glass of wine," conceded Emma.

"I always have that. No spirits. Nothing excessive."

"Andy's not drinking would be too much for us," remarked Kate after he had gone.

"I've never seen Andy the worse for drink," reassured Don. "He has a convivial personality but he drinks less alcohol than you might expect, which must stand him in good stead at conferences. He has a clearer head than some of those around him."

As they paid the hotel manager, he was looking at an account of the shooting in a morning newspaper.

"They say he was riddled with bullets."

"That sounds like a cheap novel," retorted Emma. "George wasn't cheap."

"George was her friend," whispered Don. He sought to divert her thoughts.

"The plan has been devised by someone we hardly know to be executed by someone who is not a close friend. It gives confidence."

"And," added Kate, "we're taking the treasure to sea that had been saved from the sea."

Their black humour was lost on Emma. They waited on the verandah, shaded from the hot sun, and soon heard the sound of a car, its look already becoming familiar to Kate. Mocha Joe had come alone; there would have been no room for Jim. He did clearly look at Emma to see if she were well.

"I've brought drinks for tonight and tomorrow, mineral water and fruit juice. It will be hot in the boat all day – most of the day."

"Is this going to be too much for the girls?" asked Emma, suddenly doubtful.

"No," assured Kate. "So long as it isn't too much for you."

"It will be arduous," warned Mocha Joe. "I've been out in boats in this heat. When you arrive, you'll board the train? You won't hang about in Kota Bahru?"

"Not a minute longer than we have to," said Don. "We'll be ready for home and rest. Is there anything in the boot you don't want us to see?"

"Not on this trip. Anything valuable had better go inside. You never know."

They drove from the hotel parallel to the beach.

"Could we stop here?" asked Emma. She got out of the car; the two men were intent on the road map or appeared to be; her cousins tried to look as though they were not looking at her.

"Just a minute," said Emma softly. She stood between the shop and the beach on the spot where she and George had kissed and committed the scene to memory. The sea had been over her shoulder then; she turned and looked at it; they would be going home by sea, part of the way. George would be returning to his childnood home in a coffin.

No-one spoke as they waited for Emma. Kate thought of doing so as she opened the door but even Kate felt that it was time to be quiet and patient. Mocha Joe looked round at Emma, who nodded. He drove off.

Chapter Ten

Retribution

Don was training his binoculars along the coast to the right.

"What are you looking for?" asked Ophelia.

"James's Chinese – and I think I may have found them."

"Are they waiting for us there? I thought..."

"Yes. The boat's in that inlet, hidden by overhanging branches."

Mocha Joe had driven them to a spot near the border to wait for Andy.

"I didn't expect to see him there. Bernstein. On his way to his Devil's Island. I thought he left the torturing to others – he's going back for something – the car's out of sight. He is going aboard, I think."

"Could I have a look?" He handed her the binoculars.

"I can see two men on a boat. The Chinese haven't gone. They've waited for Bernstein to pass, then come out behind him. Oh, they've guns..."

Don grabbed the binoculars, holding them away from her eyes in front of her chest for a few seconds, then slipping the lanyard over her head as she ducked. He held the binoculars to his own eyes. Ophelia thought she heard four shots, like distant thunder, two more – a pause – two – was that all?

"He's on the boat; he's been hit," said Don. "He has fallen in to the sea. You'd better not look."

Bernstein came up several times as though being water-boarded.

"Have they seen us?" asked Ophelia.

"No. Others are closer – Bernstein's men on the boat and probably more coming. The gunmen are making their getaway."

They waited a minute or two to see if anyone else was approaching from that direction before going back to the others. Ophelia's instinct was to hide when she heard a car coming, although it was from the expected side. She was hiding in bushes almost before Don missed her. He smiled.

"Do you mind if I join you? Your survival instinct is good."

As expected, it was Andy at the wheel, with James in the back, his manuscripts and jade figurines wrapped in a rug and taking up as much space as his other luggage.

"Are you taking the rug?" asked Don with a smile, gripping one side so that nothing would be tipped out.

"Where are they?" asked Andy, taking out flask after flask, leaving some in a bag on the seat, holding one in each hand. "The boat's that way," said Don.

Ophelia led them to a spot a hundred yards away, where Emma and Kate emerged from bushes. Beyond, there was a glimpse of a boat, half-concealed.

"Does hiding in bushes run in your family?" Don's tone was as jocular as the situation would allow. They approached the mooring.

"Does it look seaworthy?" asked Don.

"Did Mocha Joe think it does?"

"He did not say it doesn't." That was hardly reassuring.

They watched while Andy went closer, felt the sides, stepped aboard, went below, tinkered with the engine, started it. Kate was in the companion way when Andy switched off and turned towards her saying: "That'll do." She scampered up on to the deck as he followed her with a heavier tread but still quickly.

"It's better than it looks."

"When was it last painted?" Emma had asked on seeing the boat.

"I told you it was inconspicuous," Mocha Joe had said.

"Did you hear gunshots?" asked Andy. Kate could tell Don knew something about it, so she logically looked inquiringly at her sister.

"Bernstein has been killed," divulged Ophelia. "Don wouldn't let me look. Chinese did it, not James' s Chinese; the other lot."

"I didn't want to mention Bernstein," Don explained to Emma. "I thought it best not to say anything for a while."

"I know now. Will the police be stopping every boat?"

"I don't see why they should," said Don. "They know the killers are Chinese and have fled by land, inland, I think. It's as well they're Chinese; America is afraid to bomb China."

"Do they know the killers are Chinese?" doubted Emma. "You were looking for Chinese gangsters, so you saw them. What would his men be expecting?"

"I'm glad he's dead," burst out Kate. Seeing Don carry her gaze to Emma, she hung her head but soon afterwards muttered to Ophelia: "I'm still glad."

Their cousin's fears had not yet been allayed.

"Look, we have life-rafts," pointed out Don.

"Will they be hunting high and low?" asked Emma. "It's bad timing for us."

"It could be good timing," said Andy. "They'll be looking for Bernstein's killers; they'll be too busy to take much interest in us."

"Are we witnesses?" asked Ophelia. Don was quick to reassure her.

"You are certainly not. I don't think I am."

"Would someone come and help me carry liquid?" asked Andy. Kate and Ophelia looked at each other. "We'll both go," decided Kate.

"We must avoid dehydration," stressed Andy.

"Do you have a sunhat, Kate?" asked Emma. "Yes."

"With you?"

"Yes."

"I want you to wear it. This is no place to have sunstroke."

"Loose cotton clothes," advised Andy. "Don't expose much skin. Take plenty of liquids."

"What about your car?" asked Kate as they picked up the rest of the flasks. "Won't it look suspicious? Ought we to hide it?"

"That would look more suspicious," objected Ophelia.

"I've sold it," said Andy, "cheap. And I told the purchaser where to find it. He's Australian, so he takes such things in his stride; besides, he's a Far Eastern historian – specialises in Japan – I'm not sure what he's doing here. He's probably not sure either. He did drink my share of the wine. James got on well with him."

"He got on well with Jim," said Kate. "He's adaptable."

"Scholars often are when they raise their head from their books. I've given him a set of car keys and kept mine, immobilising the car until he picks it up."

"How far does he have to come?" asked Kate. Andy hesitated.

"We gave him a lift. There was something he wanted to see."

"Security," reminded Kate.

"Oh, he's a good bloke. He won't sell us out."

"How long have you known him?" asked Ophelia.

"I've met him a dozen times. How long have you known me – or Mocha Joe – or even Don?"

"We're good judges of character," declared Kate. "Aren't we?" Her sister agreed but tentatively.

"Anyway, the car's no problem. I hope the boat isn't. You'd better carry those in this cardboard box. Always handy, cardboard boxes."

Emma was wiping dust from the bulwarks with a bit of help from James who knew when it was best to take his cue from a woman. Don was more concerned about reaching their destination. His question to Andy was: "What does the barometer say?"

"There isn't one. I heard a weather forecast which was good. It's not the typhoon season."

"Is there a season?" asked Don warily.

Readers of Joseph Conrad know that on the high seas there is comfort in having a crimson barometer. Would it raise morale having the finest Swiss face?

"It's as flat as a millpond," said Andy with some exaggeration.

"Would these life-rafts be stout enough to repel sharks?" asked Kate.

"I wish you'd not said that."

Emma had found distraction in putting the boat to rights; now there was another worry.

"It will stay afloat until we reach shore, won't it, Andy?" Don was counting on support from the optimist.

"There's a good chance."

"How did the dinner go, James?" Don tried another tack, intent on keeping Emma's mind off George and Bernstein.

"I enjoyed it. There was an Australian who is very knowledgeable about the Far East. He told me about an alleged discovery in an Italian library of a manuscript that had been in the family for centuries. A man wrote an account of his visit to China. There's so much money to be made out of it if it were genuine. We both think it's a fake."

"A Kubla diary," observed Don.

"He thinks I'm probably right about Marco Polo's voyage but he doesn't think I'll find proof. He did say I could make an interesting book about the search."

"We'll get under way," said Andy. "Everything's aboard, isn't it?"

James opened his rug of manuscripts, jade and gems – more precious than Cleopatra. The others had a quick rummage, then gave Andy the go-ahead.

"It's all ship-shape and Bristol fashion," said Don. "They must have been a sloppy lot in London."

Kate was studying the boats, wondering which were pirates or smugglers and which innocent fishermen. A motor launch came in to view as though a submarine captain had just seen a destroyer between merchantmen.

"Police, I should think," said Andy. "Were they Thais with Bernstein, Don? No, Americans? They'll keep a low profile."

"No-one stood out as American – or European – but they were in the distance. I wasn't focusing for long. I'd guess that they were Thais. Do you know the relationship between the Thai police and the C. I. A.'s local auxiliaries?"

"I doubt if anyone does."

"You and the girls had better stay in the cabin, Emma," said Don. "James and I will make ourselves conspicuous and try to look British."

Kate and Ophelia peeped from the companionway. They watched as the launch's course brought it nearer – perhaps seventy yards away – then it curved on a course taking it north-east and out to sea.

"Is that the direction of Cambodia?" asked Don.

"Roughly," confirmed the navigator.

"Do they think the killers are off to Hong Kong by sea? They had apparently made their getaway by land."

"Would you expect Thai police to be efficient?" Andy was conversant with the ways of officialdom in south east Asia. As an afterthought: "They could be heading for Cambodia – or the police think they could."

"They could have escaped through Burma," suggested Don.

"So long as they don't come our way." Emma was sounding weary.

"You'd better lie down," said Don. She nodded. Within a few minutes she was asleep.

"It's there again," exclaimed Kate, pointing to the launch making another sweep southwards, closer to shore. "They'll be ahead of us." Briefly, it was before reversing and heading out to sea again, roughly in the direction of Cambodia.

"They're not doing it logically," criticized Andy.

"Do you think they're going through the motions?" wondered Don. "They may not care whether they catch anyone."

"Would you?"

"You surprise me, Andy. I thought you were on the side of law and order."

"Within reason."

"Mocha Joe might say that. Have you brought a gun?"

He lowered his voice. "Yes – just for safety."

"Don't tell Emma unless you have to."

Kate had overheard them, so she was sworn to secrecy.

"Have you ever been to Cambodia?" asked James, returning from the cabin with flasks of water. Ophelia was watching over Emma.

"Welcome in this heat," said Don. "T.E.Lawrence is said to have been a connoisseur of water as though it were wine. He did posture though. I've only made flying visits to Cambodia, reporting events there."

"I spent a few weeks there," said James, "roughing it when I first came out east. I wasn't the backpacking type when I was younger. Cambodia was interesting, though China gives me more to get my teeth in to. Hong Kong's the place I know best in the East: that's another China, still with its roots in old China."

"It's one of the most modern places I've seen," objected Andy.

"I mean deep down, in the backstreets."

"I wonder how much of old China ever was sleepy," mused Don. "James, I read that a man who lived in the thirteenth century left numerous progeny and his D.N.A. abounds in northern India, Aghanistan and central Asia today. Whoever has found this jumped to the conclusion that he was Genghis Khan. My first thought was that other Mongol princes and warlords will have had big harems too."

"I'm with you," said Andy.

"Maybe," said Kate, "if he was good-looking, they'd be more likely to have children and healthy children."

The men trailed in the wake of her logic.

"Because," she explained, "they'd be happy when pregnant." It dawned on them.

Fair-skinned Ophelia came on deck with sunhat dutifuly pulled down over her eyes and a cup of water to sip.

"It's getting hotter."

"Night will fall quickly," consoled her sister. Ophelia reached for the brim of Kate's hat while keeping the cup upright.

"That's better. Should we drink all the water before we drink fruit juice?"

Don deferred to Andy.

"Water, fruit juice, Indian tonic water to guard against malaria – rum only when we're running wild in port"

"Do you run wild, Andy?"

"Not really."

"So I should drink the water first," said Ophelia, "then treat myself to fruit juice. The sugar will give me energy."

"You've thought it out," acknowledged James. "You'd make a good researcher." She seemed to be turning it over in her mind.

"Emma's awake," exclaimed Kate, hearing sounds from the cabin. Sure enough, her cousin soon appeared, looking a bit queasy from falling asleep below deck. Ophelia ventured to feel Emma's forehead.

"Indian tonic water?" looking at the Old Malay Hand.

"I don't think she has malaria. A prophylactic dose would do no harm. There isn't any, Andy, is there?"

"We can buy it, once we're ashore."

"I have a miniature bottle for emergencies," said James. "You're welcome to drink that." He went searching for it in the non-treasure, non-book part of his luggage and was soon able to find it.

"If I don't have malaria," asked Emma, "will it make seasickness worse?"

"I shouldn't think so," dismissed Andy.

"I think you'll be all right," assured Don. "Drink it slowly."

"Did I hear someone talking about Genghis Khan or was I dreaming? I like Kubla Khan – the poem, that is. Coleridge claimed to have dreamt it. Am I feverish?"

"Not very," said Ophelia. "You're overwrought."

"Thank you for making that clear. I feel tired. Was Genghis Khan such a monster...as people think?"

"Yes," said Don at once, "Though not such a monster as Tamerlane. No..." he paused. "At that level, it makes no difference.'"

"I know more about Kubla than Genghis," said James. "But the family were merciless."

The Mongols had intended to spare the people of Kiev but their envoys were hanged from the battlements, so they killed everyone in the city; rioters in Kiev who oust an elected president, albeit a scoundrel, should think where violence can lead.

"Can you feel your head becoming less wuzzy?" asked Ophelia.

"Less, I think. Is it all right to eat fruit after the tonic water or should I wait?"

"I think you can eat something now," said James. It's not a strong dose of quinine." He turned to Don. "If Mocha Joe knows so much about the comings and goings of the Chinese, won't they know his boat?"

"It's not his boat. He hired it."

"They may be giving the police a wide berth," suggested Kate.

"I must phone your parents, once we're ashore in Kota Bahru," recollected Emma. "I said you were well before we left Kuala Lumpur."

"Many girls are on the phone all the time," said Andy. "It's a cordless umbilical cord."

Don set about explaining: "George Macdonald Fraser wanted to write Victorian novels; they wanted to be Victorian travellers."

"Not quite," corrected Kate. "We wanted to travel as people did before mobile phones and, in any case, we couldn't afford this trip and the smart phones we'd like. Anyway, Emma has a phone, James has a phone, I'm sure you have, Andy, with all your important appointments."

"It's not so strange," said Don. "I once knew someone who had never worn a watch, never wanted one."

"There's no shame in being Victorian," declared Ophelia. "We're all living off the ingenuity and work of Victorians."

"And Edwardians," added Kate.

"And Georgians before and Georgians after," completed Don.

"There's the police launch again," observed Andy.

They watched it come closer inshore than before, then curve away once more, this time east of the way to Cambodia.

"Will they come back?" asked Emma.

"Who knows?"

"Are there sudden squalls here?" asked James. They looked at Andy.

"It's not particularly known for that – and there are plenty of sandy beaches."

"Not particularly," repeated Don. "It could be worse. The sea's dangerous east of New Guinea, towards the Solomon Islands."

"Yes," agreed Andy. "There are salt water crocodiles."

"Seagoing crocodiles – that's not cricket,"

Ophelia was still shuddering at the thought.

"It's worse than reefs and cannibals."

"You're not going to be eaten by anything or anyone," comforted Kate.

"The cannibals are long gone," said Don, "some gave up surprisingly late. The end of the nineteenth century, Andy?"

"A few of them clung to old ways. About that date, I should think. It had been part of their culture for so long."

"Where exactly are we going to land?" asked Emma. "Is it marked on the map you were given?"

Andy held out the coastal map Mocha Joe had given them.

"So we're about here," worked out Emma, moving her finger parallel to the coast. "And the boat will be beached, not tied to a landing-stage. Then we'll have to transport our luggage to the railway station. I'm feeling tired at the thought."

Don took the map from her. He knew Kota Bahru better than she, so the details of the map meant more. He was able to picture hotels along the sea-front, the way to the railway station, Kota Bahru's increasingly Moslem aspect.

"All we have to worry about is Andy's navigation," he whispered.

Emma was still looking off colour, incipient sea-sickness and worries about the landing feeding on each other. Kate urged her to drink a special mixture of fruit juices concocted by herself in the galley.

"Not many miles to go," said Andy, coming up after checking how much fuel was left in the tank. "We'll get there."

"And soon," said Don. "The light's just beginning to fade."

Ophelia looked askance with her younger, artist's eyes, suspecting that he was merely trying to cheer them up, but a few minutes later she did feel that day was on the wane.

"I haven't noticed him letting out knots," observed Kate, who liked to know where she stood with maritime practices.

"Boats have moved on," said Ophelia. "This is old-fashioned without satellite navigation."

"Does it measure speed accurately, so that we know when to head for land? And what if there's a sand bank?"

"The boat has a shallow draught," assured Andy. "Rocks would have been marked on the chart. We can cope with a bit of sand."

Ophelia put her head on one side in silent scepticism.

"The landing-place does seem to be as near to the railway station as possible," said Kate "Mocha Joe is thoughtful," she added, giving him his due.

"He is," agreed Don. "He may be a criminal but he's thoughtful."

"I wish this boat were better appointed," said Emma. "There's no freshwater for a shower."

"We could dip a bucket in the sea," suggested Kate. "If there is a bucket," she added doubtfully. "There must be."

Emma drew the line at standing naked like Captain Hornblower while buckets of seawater were dashed over her.

"Why don't you wait until we're close to shore?" asked Don, "then swim the last ten yards? You'll feel refreshed."

"I hope we don't all have to swim the last ten yards," said Andy, overhearing the discussion. "I've done a bit of tacking, which has left the petrol low."

"Why were you tacking?" James was not in a mood to wade ashore with his valuables.

"To confuse people, so they would not be sure where we were going."

"We are going to make it though, Andy?"

"I think so, give or take wet feet."

The light was now certainly fading. Kate looked in what she thought was the direction of the railway station. Somewhere beyond lay Kuala Lumpur.

"Escaping's exhilirating, whatever you're escaping from." Don's words made them feel they were well on their way home.

Soon afterwards, Emma and the girls greeted Malaysian waters, entering Kota Bahru in bikinis without knowing quite where the decorum police stood on that.

"Bounce the bow on the water," said Andy, "and she'll come up on to the sand."

They tried several times, finding it quite enjoyable, and, at length, timed it well enough.

"We need a mooring-ring," said Don. "Should there be one? I can't see any other boats at present." A man who had been watching them beach the boat came closer, which would have been alarming, had he been in uniform, not long, loose shirt and trousers, probably sailor's or fishermen's garb.

"Are you Mr. Ashdown, sir?"

"Yes," said Andy, singled out as being in charge.

"I was told to look after the boat."

"I'm glad he thought of that. Is it your boat we've borrowed?"

"No. It belongs to my cousin."

"How do we stop it floating off?" asked Don.

"By dragging her a bit higher," explained the newcomer. "Could you help me do that? Usually, she's beached where there is a mooring-ring."

"But this is nearer to the railway station?" surmised Kate.

"Yes. There will be a crew to take her out."

With some exertion, they managed to drag the boat higher, Kate joining in and complaining: "We don't have the weight to lever it."

"Rollers would help," said Andy. "If there's a high tide, she'll float off."

"She won't be here long."

"You may have been paid," said Don, "but I'd like you to have this as well. Malaysian notes?"

"Many thanks." The man smiled.

They prepared for the long haul. Mocha Joe had provided two baskets, which might appear to contain fishing-tackle – and had probably contained firearms.

"Too cumbersome?" suggested Emma.

They decided it would be best to leave the treasure in the trusty hessian bags; there would not be a smell of fishing tackle so there would be no point in carrying the baskets to the railway station.

"We need a porter who isn't fleetfooted," said Don, "one who can't run off with valuables." Emma tried to smile.

It was wearisome work lugging their bags in a still very warm evening. Emma and the girls had dried off quickly before dressing.

"It's a pity it's not cold enough to wear more clothes," lamented Kate.

What revived them was the sight of what looked like a railway station. Don reconnoitered ahead, signalling that they were on the right track. A porter offered his services. Don looked him over and decided he was slow enough. The porter was no match for those in Darjeeling or Shimla but he was able to relieve the travellers of much of their burden, the men insisting that he lighten Emma's load first, then that of the girls, who had the vigour of youth but were slightly built. Andy, of course, remained the most robust.

"Will there be a buffet at the station?" asked Kate.

"There must be. I have to tell your parents that all is well, so I need to sound as though it is."

"You need a sit-down and a drink," said Don.

When Emma had found her phone and drunk relaxing tea and collected herself, she keyed in her code. She had been trying to put her best face on her bereavement; now it was her best voice.

"Think of Laurel and Hardy," urged Don.

"They'll wonder why I'm laughing."

"Think of seeing Hazel and Dewey again," said Ophelia.

"Ye...s," Emma sighed with relief. Once she was talking, she was at ease.

"I'm sure it will do them good," she was saying. "They've adapted well and they've met some interesting people. (aside) Andy, try to sound interesting."

"They're delightful girls. I'm dealing with cynical businessmen much of the time, so it's a change to meet freshness and openness to new experience."

"Don't stress that," interrupted Emma.

"They've seen east and west coasts of Malaysia, Kuala Lumpur..."

"A rubber plantation," prompted Emma.

"A rubber plantation," repeated Andy. "And...they've heard some fine music."

Emma took the phone again.

"They want to speak to you. Don't give much away; it's too complicated."

"You're beginning to think like a teenage girl," whispered Kate.

"I was one," reminded Emma.

They managed to sound untroubled without being suspiciously chirpy. It was the first time on the trip their parents had heard from them, so Emma waited for them to have a good natter before taking the phone again.

"They say you seem to be getting a lot out of the trip," she passed on.

"You were taking a chance with Andy," said Don. "You should have given me a chance to sound interesting."

"Do you feel homesick after talking to your parents?" The girls looked at each other, Emma's question causing them to wonder what they did feel.

"A bit," said Kate, "no, we're going to feel homesick when it's time but that's not yet. We'd still like to travel some more." Ophelia nodded.

"Have you found the train, Andy?" asked Don.

"There's one in fifteen minutes. We'd better make our way to the platform."

He had made a note of the time and platform just to be certain. The porter had been on standby. For a tip reflecting their tiredness, he was happy to help carry their luggage to the platform for Kuala Lumpur.

"When I get home," said Don, "I'll sleep for a week."

"You won't," disagreed Kate.

Chapter Eleven

An Unexpected Meeting

At length, they deposited all their luggage in an empty compartment. Kate drifted in and out of sleep and was vaguely aware of her sister doing the same. Andy and Don had discovered the advisability of someone keeping watch without breathing a word of the reason for it. James went looking for a dining car, found one and returned to say that breakfast would be served; there was nothing available yet so late at night.

"I'm too tired to eat," said Ophelia.

"Have we missed much by not spending a day in Kota Bahru?" asked Kate.

"Hazel would say no. She doesn't like the place."

In Kota Bahru, they had remembered what Hazel had said about schoolgirls having to wear traditional dress. Islam was adopted in the East Indies in the sixteenth century. Was it established earlier in the Malayan peninsula? Before then, traditional dress would probably have meant girls being bare-breasted, as in Bali in the nineteen sixties and much of southern India in the eighteenth century.

Was it nearly dawn, wondered Kate. Lights from buildings were confusing. She heard Don speaking in an undertone: "Richard could help you; his bank will have a deposit box." Then...footsteps along the corridor. Don stopped speaking.

"Breakfast is served in the dining car," announced an attendant. Kate stood up, prodded her sister gently and sat down again. Ophelia's eyes opened as she registered sound and prod. Kate summoned the energy to stand up and find her purse. Emma was still drowsy.

146

"Would you like us to bring you tea and sandwiches?" asked Kate.

"Yes please. Whatever looks tasty."

"Malaysian? Because you're nearly home."

It was a smaller dining car than on the Orient Express and there was probably less choice. As they were looking over the drinks and sandwiches, Kate glanced towards the tables and saw Mocha Joe. He had been watching them, waiting with a smile for them to see him.

"So all went well."

"Did Jim put out to sea to keep an eye on us?"

"No. There are several fishermen I know along this stretch of coast."

"You knew which train we'd be catching."

"That was easy enough to estimate."

"For some people."

He turned to Ophelia.

"I have a request." He seemed more uncertain than they had seen him.

"Would you draw a portrait of your sister and another of yourself? I have a shaving-mirror that might help,"

"You don't seem to have used it much," Kate could not prevent herself from saying. Ophelia's shoulder-bag contained not only her money but her sketch book, as he had probably guessed.

"I'll be happy to do that. I don't know what we'd have done without you."

"Have a drink first. Coffee?" She nodded.

"To wake me up." He turned to the attendant, passing on their order.

"Emma would like something Malaysian," said Kate.

"Very Malaysian?"

"I don't know."

"This should be safe. Blame me if it isn't."

Emma welcomed the sandwiches with no thought as to who had chosen them.

"Ophelia's in the dining-car drawing for someone."

"Drawing someone?"

"For someone. I have to go back to pose. It would be when I'm a wreck."

Kate enjoyed Emma's being intrigued.

"I'll drink this tea then come with you. It sometimes seems that true Darjeeling is a thing of the past; bags don't have the aroma of loose leaf Darjeeling. I'll have to shift my affections."

Their eyes met momentarily; neither spoke of George.

"That's not Darjeeling, is it?"

"Who knows what it is? It's got me thinking about tea,"

If Emma had been wideawake, she would have guessed who was in the dining-car. James could have told her as he made himself comfortable, with manuscript and food concealing valuables from the casual passer-by. Don took his turn to stretch his legs and seek refreshment. Mocha Joe stood at Ophelia's shoulder watching the portrait take shape.

"We met when she was drawing me."

"I'm proud to say she has drawn a portrait of me. We're brothers under the pencil.

"Pastel makes more finished portraits than pencil," said Ophelia. "It brings out the highlights."

"You're vain," chided Don. "Colour for you but not for us. It's sexism."

"Very like," said Andy, appearing behind Ophelia. "Could you have drawn your reflection in a glass of champagne and called it conviviality?"

To Mocha Joe he said: "The boat was satisfactory, ideal for undercover work."

"I think I can beat that. When I need to."

"We saw Thai police making a show of hot pursuit."

"That's what I'd expect of them."

Ophelia remembered that he had supplied arms to the opposition.

"Where have you been, Andy?" asked Don. "You came here, then you were back in the compartment; you were gone; I was in the corridor a few minutes ago. How did you pass me?"

"I was up and down the train, looking for suspicious characters."

"You're one and our friend here is another."

"Were you half-asleep standing up, Don?" suggested Ophelia.

"I am awake now. I think. You're not in my dream."

"She would enrich dreams," said Andy.

Mocha Joe may have thought that but did not speak out. Fatigue was forgotten as Ophelia's hand danced over the paper.

"Look who's here," said Kate as they entered the dining car.

"I thought you might turn up. Thank you again for helping us."

"I've done little – but it's a little good."

"Are you going to get off just before Kuala Lumpur?" asked Kate, "as you got off just before Bangkok?"

"You never know."

"Is your hand tired?" asked Emma, tired herself.

"Was I asking too much?" Mocha Joe was uneasy but not regretful.

"I've got my second wind now," insisted the artist.

"You don't have to flatter yourself," ventured Mocha Joe.

"I'll need to flatter Kate though."

"You won't."

"I risked phoning Dewey and Hazel," said Emma.

"When did you do that?" asked Kate.

"When you were asleep."

"But we thought we were awake longer than you were."

"It's quality that counts. I haven't gone in to detail but I've told them where and when the train will arrive."

"I suggested to James that he call on Richard," said Don.

"At once?" asked Andy. "He could be busy, could be away." James looked worried, afraid that it would all go wrong at the last minute.

"Hazel saw Richard yesterday," reassured Emma, "and he's planning another soirée. He pays music students to perform," she explained to Mocha Joe.

"Livelier than you might think," informed Andy. "There was dancing afterwards, probably will be next time. You can throw yourself about."

"I can vouch for that," confirmed Kate.

"You?"

"No. Andy."

"He's only been once," said Emma, "We're regulars."

"More melodious than this," added Don. "Pity there's no Sinatra," he said, luring Mocha Joe in to revealing his musical taste.

"I enjoy Sinatra."

"You would," observed Emma, "It's singing for people who've been around, who have known life's ups and downs."

"After a down there's always the chance of an up." Don smiled approvingly, mouthing: "yes" behind Emma's back.

"Did you...tell Hazel...?"

"Not over the phone." Don saw the logic of her answer.

"Have you had enough to eat?" asked Kate. "Can I find something to tempt you?"

"I'll have another of these."

"Mocha Joe chose that. He's well up in Malaysian cuisine."

"Have you been here longer than I have then?"

"Probably. Seeing the region from different angles."

"Where do you go on holiday?" asked Kate. "Do you have holidays?"

"Singapore, Kuala Lumpur, Sydney."

"I can picture you on the Gold Coast," said Don. "Still more I can picture Andy on the Gold Coast."

"I've been there," he confirmed, "several times."

Ophelia handed Mocha Joe the portrait of herself. He did not say he would treasure it; he did not need to. He looked at it attentively with an air that suggested he would be looking at it the same way in years to come.

"Is that what you wanted?" asked Don.

"Yes. Lovely and thoughtful."

Kate sat down to sit for her portrait.

"How good is the paper?"

"Good enough."

"Do you know your sister better than you know yourself?" asked Don.

"Perhaps. I've known her a long time."

"I'll give James a spell," said Andy. "And see who else is on the train."

"A secret agent manqué," observed Don.

James arrived full of his book.

"I don't suppose you'll give me an address, so that I can send you a copy of my book when it is published?"

"I'm hard to pin down."

"Would you give me a holiday address? In Australia?"

"He goes there," confirmed Kate.

Mocha Joe paused, then nodded. He wrote an address on a slip of paper.

"Guard it with your life," he joked. James returned to the compartment to put the address with his other valuables.

"I like Adelaide," said Mocha Joe. "Does that surprise you?"

"It pleases me. Adelaide and Sinatra make you a more rounded smuggler."

Don was keeping an eye on Emma as he talked, glancing inquiringly at her cup. She shook her head.

"Do you feel an affinity with Humphrey Bogart?" asked Ophelia, fleetingly looking up from her drawing.

"Who? No. I have seen a few. Would you think me vain if I said yes? You would." She smiled, enjoying getting to know him better.

Kate wanted the drawing to take a long time because she began to feel Mocha Joe was about to leave and she wanted him to stay longer.

As the morning progressed, a few more people came in to the dining car without disturbing Ophelia's concentration.

"She can draw anywhere," said Kate proudly.

"Keep still."

Andy returned to snatch a bite before Kuala Lumpur.

"James is double checking everything. He's afraid of leaving something important on the train. I was thinking about Thailand. There could be all out civil war in a few years' time."

"If someone took sides, he'd very soon become disillusioned and want to pack it in," surmised Kate. She could tell by his face that her guess had hit home, and he did not give much away.

"You could be safer writing your memoirs?" advised Andy.

"I'd not have much to tell."

"That's hard to believe," said Emma, meeting his eyes directly.

"I'll stay on the train to Kuala Lumpur, then slip away quickly. I'll go and fetch my things."

When he had gone, Emma asked a question that had been on her mind:

"How did the Chinese know where to find Bernstein? Did Mocha Joe tell them?"

"I wondered about that," said Don. "It's best not to ask."

"You're right," agreed Emma. "If he was involved, I'd rather not know."

"But you understand the motives he would have had for a hypothetical setting up?"

"Ye...s." Emma looked glum. She would not have been one for realpolitik.

"He has helped us. Remember that."

"I shall. I'd like to think of him as a friend. That's why I'd rather he were not involved in..."

"Shady dealings? I think they're shady rather than nefarious. If he were evil, would he have asked for those portraits?"

Don broke off as Mocha Joe came in to view along the corridor, carrying a plain shoulder bag and a smarter valise.

"You're travelling light," observed Emma.

"I usually do. Except when I'm going to stay somewhere for a month or two. I'm picking things up in Kuala Lumpur."

"Are we going to see Richard tonight?" asked Andy. "James would like to."

"I'd like to go home now," said Emma, "and see him tomorrow."

"That's right," encouraged Kate. "You'll feel better after a night in your own bed."

For a moment, Emma seemed to be wondering which was the teacher and which the seventeen-year-old. Mocha Joe looked amused by the incongruity, then straightened his face.

"I think I've made as much of Kate as I can," declared Ophelia.

"Surely not," teased Don. "She calls for a few more flourishes."

"No." Ophelia was firm. "It's finished. What do you think?" she asked the drawing's recipient. His smile showed satisfaction.

"I like them very much. Have you excelled yourself?"

"She's always good," praised Kate. "And she'll get better – as you might see for yourself in a few year's time."

Emma frowned. It was too near to an invitation for her liking. She was still wary of welcoming Mocha Joe as a bosom friend.

He put the two drawings in his valise between sheets of paper and what looked like silk. Knowing the approach to Kuala Lumpur, he was able to order a last cup of green tea and a round of assorted drinks for his companions.

"It's a pity we can't invite Mocha Joe to the soirée," whispered Kate mischievously.

"You never know, he might like Mozart," supported Ophelia.

"Does he keep open house?" asked Mocha Joe, catching their words.

"Not for you," regretted Kate. "More's the pity."

They picked up their drinks from the counter and Mocha Joe raised his tea in an unspoken toast to the party, which first Don, then the others answered without voicing a compliment. He shook hands with Kate, Ophelia and Emma in turn, careful not to crush their hands, the girls' grip lingering.

"We'll think of you when we see Bogart," said Ophelia.

"I'll think of me when I see Bogart."

"Thanks for looking after us," said Emma, "smuggler, gun-runner, Good Samaritan."

"Many things to some women." He acknowledged the complexity and subtlety of their relationship.

"We're nearly there. I hope all goes well for you." The train was slowing. He turned to them, smiling, as he gripped the door handle and the train came to a stop.

Don's parting words to him were:

"It's funny how you meet and drift."

"There's Dewey," said Emma. "And Hazel." The train had overrun them.

"Who was that?" asked Dewey. "You like him."

"Do we?" asked Kate. Dewey realised they were not going to be forthcoming, so she turned to Don. "Who was that walking away?"

"He's probably incognito. The girls met him on a train to Thailand."

Hazel saw by Emma's face that something was wrong.

"What is it? You're all here and look well enough."

"George Berson has been killed – by Chinese gangsters, who mistook him for Bernstein, who had used him as a decoy. They did kill Bernstein soon afterwards."

Hazel kissed her, then held her by both shoulders as though steadying her for life's tribulations.

"George? Dead?" exclaimed Dewey as though Berson had no business dying when he was likeable. She looked glumly at the girls, angrily at a building opposite as the injustice of it began to sink in.

Hazel noticed James, the man who thought her too old for treasure-hunting.

"Treasure? Did you find any?"

"Yes," said James, glad to be vindicated.

"Much?"

"Quite a bit," assessed Don.

"Right. I'll be with you in two shakes of a Iamb's tail. Bear with me." And she was off in her somewhat incongruous sports car, old enough to be hired cheap whenever she was in Kuala Lumpur.

"I'll find a taxi," said Andy. "Are you in the same hotel, James?"

"I'm not booked in. I didn't know how long we'd be away."

"I should be able to sort that out, get you in somewhere. I'm invited to a party tonight. You can come along if you're at a loose end."

"Amazing," murmured Don. "I wish I had his stamina."

Dewey hugged Emma, then turned back to looking angrily at the traffic. Don watched Andy trying to hail a taxi.

"Should Dewey go home with you?"

"The girls are all I need tonight."

"Be proud," whispered Don. "She's comfortable with you."

"She's comfortable with you, Don."

"Not in the same way."

"We can't all fit in one taxi, can we?" Kate clearly thought not.

"There's no-one fat," said Ophelia. "And some taxis are big."

"Hazel wants us to wait for her," reminded Don, "which is a complication if Andy stops a taxi in the next few minutes."

"We could start walking the way Hazel went," suggested Kate.

"Hazel's ways can be unpredictable," quipped Don.

"We're all too tired." Emma was firm on that.

Andy had just stopped a taxi when Hazel came in to sight.

"Get in, James," she commanded. "With all your luggage. We're going straight to Richard's. He wants to see the rest of you as soon as you're up to it."

And off they went in the sports car, leaving the others to decide who were going to sit in the seats facing the back, normally taken by children in a wedding party. As juniors, the girls were chosen, along with Andy, who prided himself on being adaptable.

"Hazel gave me a lift and abandoned me," grumbled Dewey. "She took James instead." Being dumped for James made it worse.

"He has something for you," said Kate. "A present. Just what you'll like."

"You're not going to tell me what it is."

"No." Kate shook her head. Emma was able to smile.

"It'll be a surprise, Dewey. You'll enjoy it more," Don assured her.

"I'll enjoy it as much as it pleases my taste. And he doesn't know my taste. A scholar deceiving a librarian," she recalled. What was the world coming to?

"You'll think differently when you see him, Dewey," said Don.

"Are we going to the coffee-house?" asked Kate.

"Why not?" asked Andy. Emma raised her eyebrows, then thought again.

"We did get some sleep on the train. A bath will revive me."

"We'll be there as soon as possible." Kate took it upon herself to speak for the three of them.

Emma kept her promise to herself, luxuriating in a bath, which washed over the heartache but did not wash it away. They were first to the coffee house, which already seemed familiar, and approved of its coffee, mellow and reviving, just the thing after a long journey. Don looked well enough when he arrived, just before a busy Dewey, carrying shopping. What surprised them was to see Hazel and James arrive, not quite arm in arm but talking amicably, fast friends it seemed. James had an attaché case.

"There you are," said Kate to Dewey. James took out three books.

"I want you to choose one, for yourself, not your library, to make up for going there under false pretences. You may see now why it was so important."

Dewey softened; and her eyes lit up as she examined the books.

"I can't decide at once. I'll tell you in half an hour, when we're ready to go."

James opened the case before Emma, inviting her to choose.

"A gem for a gem," said Don warmly.

"Will you want it to go with all your clothes?" asked Ophelia.

"That's not easy. Most of them, maybe."

"Here's Andy," said Kate.

"Has he found you somewhere to sleep, James?" asked Don.

"I've managed to get a room in the same hotel. For two nights, then away to Australia to divvy up with my partner."

"Brooch or pendant?" asked Dewey. "You must decide which. A chain's easy. I know where you can get a stone set in a brooch quickly – and skilfully."

"A blue brooch would go well with the yellow pendant," said Ophelia gently. Emma smiled at her tone of voice.

"You choose for me; you have an artist's eye." Perhaps it would mean more because her cousin had chosen it.

"Is this a sapphire? It's not big but it's pretty."

"In a brooch," suggested James. Emma nodded.

"Ophelia would like a peridot," said Kate.

"She shall have a peridot." He had anticipated her wish.

"Kate wants a big pearl and all sorts of stones to set it off," announced her sister. Emma looked askance.

"Would a medium-sized pearl do?" James held it out.

"Oh, yes," answered Kate, embarrassed at being thought greedy.

"That's more than enough. I was talking about what I had dreamt of, not what I expected you to give me."

"I know," said James. "You must have something, Don."

"I've never been one for jewellery. I leave it to the fairer sex."

"A black spinel, Don? Two or three on a tie-pin or as collar-studs or cuff-links?"

"I think you should have a tie-pin," opined Kate. "Black would be distinguished, discreet, matching your personality."

"The Black Spinel sounds like a master criminal. Yes, I could wear a tie-pin; I wear a tie quite often."

"Three, I think," decided James. One might look lonely; three might have more effect."

"How will you wear the peridot?" Emma asked her cousin.

"On a simple chain for the time being."

"I must have several in my jewellery box; there's not much else, alas."

"You should treat yourself."

"I do. To clothes."

"Andy should have something from the sea," said Ophelia.

"A recipe for cooking seaweed? It was fun. A seashell would be a memento of the trip. I wasn't in from the start. I'm happy to have helped out."

"Richard's being helpful too," said James. "We've taken most of the jade to a deposit-box in his bank."

"And you want the rest," presumed Don. "I've hidden it under Miles Davis; only a jazz-loving burglar would look there. Where are you goiing to sell it? And the paintings?"

"I know a few diplomats who might fancy them," said Andy, "unless...when is Richard retiring to Australia?"

"Very soon, I think," said Hazel. "I don't know why. Does Australia have anything that's not here?"

Don was giving that some thought but did not take the matter up with her immediately.

"So we'd better take everything to Richard's?" asked Emma, "or give it to you, James? Is your hotel room safe?"

"Not as safe as Richard's bank – or his house."

"Will he be there this evening?"

"He will tomorrow," said Hazel. "There's a recital. You're all invited. He said he's looking forward to Andy's dancing."

"It's an art form," commented Don, straight-faced.

Dewey plumped for the photographs.

"I like that for the binding but there are so many people in here and their homes, shops, offices, churches, temples. It gives a glimpse of their lives. It sets me thinking." She looked kindly on James now.

"Will you sell the other books in Australia," asked Andy. "There will be people from Indo-China – and China."

"Probably," answered James. "I'll ask my partner's opinion. She will certainly want to see them before sale."

"She'll be pleased with the results of your expedition," said Don.

"Are you going to the party, James?" asked Emma.

"Yes," said the unbridled scholar. "Would you like to come?"

"No, thanks. The soirée is more my style."

"Don?"

"The same. I'm tired anyway. I doubt if the wine will be as good as Richard's. I like quality in all things. I prefer "Blue Monk" to Blue Nun."

"The drink won't be too bad," reassured Andy, "and there'll be conversation – and ladies."

"There are ladies here," pointed out Dewey, "and will be tomorrow."

"You haven't finished your drink, Dewey," said Emma. "Are you going to have anything to eat?"

"I'm not in the mood – a new book's still exciting when it's special, like this."

"You've put it away now. You can eat."

"I still don't feel like it." Kate looked amused.

"You're worried about Dewey not eating and we're worried about you not eating – or sleeping – and Don can't live by Miles Davis alone."

Dewey had her cold coffee topped up.

"If you give me those gems, I'll have them set for you before the soirée."

Emma handed hers over, so Kate followed suit.

"Easy come, easy go," said Kate. "We'll have to wear our best dresses again. Everyone's seen them."

"What an imposition, having to wear your best. You'll have new jewellery though. That's what women will notice if it's women you're worried about."

"Should we wear black?"

"A little if you like but I want you to enjoy yourselves and look as though you're enjoying yourselves. Why does Hazel love the city? Think about that."

"When do you have to be back at school?" asked Ophelia.

"In a week."

"You need a holiday. Could you ask for more time off?"

"It would leave them short-staffed."

Ophelia thought of mentioning compassionate leave; it reminded her:

"You need to send a card of condolence to George's family. We'll help you choose it and we'll all sign it to let them know how many people here liked him and are missing him."

"Very well," said Emma. "We'll go as soon as I've finished my coffee. Dewey's off in a minute." The librarian had stood up and was checking that the new book was snug in her bag.

"I can picture Dewey," said Kate, "in a tee-shirt with Jacky Chan kicking Father Ted." There was a hint of a smile from Emma.

Hazel heard of their errand with approval; Don was talking to Andy about the F.B.I. getting more information than the C.I.A. without torture.

"That's their claim."

The soirée was to start earlier than last time and they were there in good time with the paintings to give to Richard for safe keeping.

"How big an art collection does Mocha Joe have?" wondered Emma. "Will those portraits be a good influence on him as meeting you has surely been?"

Chapter Twelve

In The Steps Of Micawber

Kate had tried to trick out her dress with a ribbon or two but was waiting eagerly and hopefully for Dewey. Ophelia was already wearing her peridot on a chain Emma had given her and the ear-rings she had bought in Bangkok. Emma's dress was grey, dashed with purple, rich rather than sombre, matching, she hoped, the tone of the evening.

"That scarf's perfect," approved Kate, chafing a bit at not having the perfect ensemble herself.

"Here she is," exclaimed Emma. "I knew she wouldn't let us down."

Dewey's face told them she had been successful. She held up a purse but did not risk opening it until she reached them. The sapphire and pearl had been set in silver at Hong Kong speed. Kate felt a new girl. Emma hugged Dewey for knowing how she could help and when.

"I'll pin it on for you." Meticulously, the librarian selected the best spot for the brooch. Kate was putting hers on herself when Ophelia took a hand, adjusting it infinitesimally, it seemed to Kate.

"That looks right," approved Emma. She caught sight of Hazel approaching, on foot as usual for short distances, so went to meet her. The others were drifting towards the doorway when Richard appeared, quickening their steps.

"I'm glad to welcome you home from your adventure," said Richard. "How is Emma bearing up?"

"As well as might be expected." Kate instinctively felt her brooch, recalling Emma seeking the comfort of her amber pendant.

"I feel as though I'd known George much longer than I did," said Ophelia. "Likeable people can make an impression quickly."

"I thought it best to play Bach tonight," explained Richard. "It will take her out of herself in the best sense."

He welcomed them in to the recital room, where Don was already waiting, this time in a black suit, not navy blue, black. His tie was deep blue with hints of green. Dewey walked up to him, seized his tie and took out a newly made black spinel tie-pin. When she had fastened it to her satisfaction, she stood back to admire her handiwork, that of the chosen jeweller, and the model.

"I've liked black suits since I saw them in Spain. This seemed as good an occasion as any to wear one. The ensemble matches the tie-pin."

"I thought you liked ice-blue," recalled Ophelia.

"I do. That's my favourite but you will allow me to wear black sometimes. Sophistication is not altogether foreign to me."

"Blue can be sophisticated."

"You're being difficult. Very pretty but difficult."

"Have you brought your records?"

"You enjoyed them? Good."

Richard was greeting Andy, open-necked as usual; Dewey would not tie him down with a tie-pin.

"Has Andy mellowed since we met him?" asked Kate, "or have we mellowed?"

"You, you mean?"

"Emma will think you're in mourning," whispered Ophelia.

"I'd not thought of that. Tell Richard I'll be back soon; I'll slip out the back."

He was gone before Emma could see him.

This time Dewey's cheongsam was red, embroidered in gold, with tiny dragons in the hem as though they were breathing fire on her legs to keep them warm. Festive in her attire, she was vengeful towards those responsible for George's death.

"Bernstein and the C.I.A. set him up," said Kate.

"They should be hunted down," declared Dewey, determined as Thomas Dewey, who trapped Lucky Luciano, boss of the Mafia, and gaoled him for a long term. Franklin Roosevelt's government did a deal with the Mafia to facilitate the landing in Sicily. The best thing Mussolini did was to suppress the Mafia. The American government released hundreds of Mafiosi and gave them control of local government in Sicily. Luciano was also released and sent back to Italy. Few Italians were happy about this.

"Did I hear that you're at war with America?" asked Andy.

"Only a bit of it."

"The one who was most guilty has paid," pointed out Ophelia. Dewey stopped to think about that.

"What music did George like?" asked Kate.

"You'd have to ask Emma but you can't ask Emma; you'd touch a raw nerve."

"It might do her good to have happy memories of something they had in common," argued Kate. Ophelia seemed unconvinced.

"Where's Don gone?" asked Richard.

"He'll be back soon," said Ophelia uncertainly. White lies did not come naturally to her. "I think he forgot something."

Hazel and Emma entered, Richard greeting them warmly.

"Look what James gave me," invited Hazel. "He chose well." The eye travelled from the pale yellow citrine to a Krugerrand.

"She's friends with James now," observed Emma. "It would have been a bit much for you, Hazel. A long boat trip, then carrying all our luggage to the railway station."

"You must tell me more of the details," said Richard. "James left a lot out."

"There are things Kate knows better than James," replied Emma. "Her scrapes. Did you hear about Madame Sir?"

"Not much."

"I'll tell you then. She's interesting – and has a few things in common with you. She's retiring soon, leaving south-east Asia."

"One scrape," grumbled Kate as her elders moved away in conversation.

"James is late." Dewey sounded severe. She still had it in for the C.I.A.

"We're starting early, aren't we?" said Hazel. "He probably doesn't know."

Don returned in a velvety beige jacket and fawn trousers, his tie and white shirt unchanged.

"Now you're fit for Emma's eyes." He had Ophelia's approval.

"That was a quick change," remarked Dewey.

"He looked as though he was in mourning," whispered Ophelia.

"I prefer this outfit, Don," decided Dewey. "And I like you in blue."

"Stick to what works," Don admonished himself. "The girl in a dragon dress has spoken. Is red thought lucky all over east Asia?"

"Lucky, worn by me; lucky for the onlookers. I don't know how widespread the belief is. You know I'm half-hearted about Feng Shui and I'm not superstitious about colours. I'm a modern person – but one who enjoys the classics."

Kate too was wearing red.

"Kate must be lucky," said Ophelia. "Or is it only while she's in the East?".

"Colours are the same the world over."

"No. They're not. Perceptions of them change according to the light."

"You like gold, don't you, Hazel?" remarked Ophelia. "It suits you and it goes well with the citrine."

"I don't only wear gold," said Hazel. "I buy pewter covered with silver from Malaysia."

"Before Emma comes back," confided Andy. "I talked to one of my contacts today. They've no particular lead to Bernstein's killers, except that they are assumed to be Chinese. They'll most likely give it up as a bad job and move on."

"Has Bernstein left any files..." Don lowered his voice, "on the girls and..."

"As far as I can tell, nothing that's being pursued. Are you in a mood to kick your heels up, Dewey?"

"I'm always in a mood to let myself go, within reason."

"That's Dewey," said Don. "And Emma too," he added softly.

"Did I hear you saying the Americans aren't after us," asked Kate.

"We'd not allowed for young ears, Andy. It seems like it. You have to watch out for the British as well, of course. I think a Libyan was arrested here and handed over to Gadaffi. But you don't need to worry about the British."

Emma's return was punctuated by her slowing every two or three steps to sip a glass of wine Richard had given her.

"You'll be listening to your classics soon, Dewey," said Don, observing Richard enter with the two students they recognised from the previous recital and a girl carrying a violin.

"James," recognised Kate. "Is there a spring in his step?"

"There isn't in mine yet," said Emma. "I need to sit down and listen to beautiful music. You won't find it easy to get me dancing, Don."

"A slow waltz?"

"If someone holds me up."

"I'm on the right lines now," declared James. "I'll start the book with my dream and the search; even if I don't find what I'm after, it won't matter; there'll still be a story."

"A story can take you a long way," encouraged Don.

"But you do want to prove you're right," said Kate acutely.

"Yes. That's what I'm aiming for."

"Still the scholar." Don looked pleased at his perseverance.

"Is there a programme?" asked Hazel.

"Printed?" queried Dewey. "I haven't seen one. We'd better take our seats. There seem to be more people than last time."

"Will you draw the recital afterwards?" Emma asked her cousin.

"Probably. To fix it in my memory. That plump woman, she talked to us last time, didn't she?"

"Yes. You'll find her name hard to remember but don't call her plump to her face – or to her friends."

They took their seats, Richard saying as he passed; "It begins with the Bach Siciliano, the one Loussier played." Don looked approving.

The girl pianist composed herself, hands poised above the keyboard. Neither of the girls had heard the music. Don watched their faces, reading their response, as they watched, alternately, the pianist and a soothed Emma. The trio next played their arrangement of "Sheep may safely graze". "I remember a student teacher of music who said there is no emotion in Bach," said Emma, incredulous.

"There is nothing more deeply emotional than Bach." Don had no doubts on that score. The violinist next played the main theme from Zhang Yimou's "Hero", the pianist a late Mozart sonata.

"The flautist will feel left out," said Kate as the musicians acknowledged applause at the interval. "Perhaps the girls are ganging up on him."

The woman who could not be called plump was between them and the refreshments, apparently pleased to renew their acquaintance.

"Better not say much about Thailand," counselled Don.

"We've been seeing the sights," replied Kate when plied with questions. "There's so much here and in the rest of Malaysia." She felt more comfortable when she caught up with Hazel.

"Have you ever worn golden pearls?" occurred to her.

"No. I like pearls to look like pearls; that's not my sort of gold."

"Is it your sort of music?"

"Yes. I'm enjoying it."

"Do you time your visits to coincide with the recitals?"

"I try to but I don't know the exact dates in advance."

Emma was holding a glass again, so Kate hurried to her side.

"They're very good for students, aren't they? It feels friendly here: a big concert hall doesn't have the same atmosphere."

"It's not wine this time," said Emma, answering her thoughts rather than her words. "Richard suggested this. Dewey says there are twelve ingredients and that's a lucky number for a festival drink."

"She believes in lucky numbers?"

"She may have been joking; she sounded serious. If people are watching what I drink, are they watching what you drink?"

"I am," said Ophelia.

"I'm booking a dance, Emma," said Andy as he passed on his way to talk to some dignitary before turning his attention to James. Andy's latest project was to get James published as soon as possible. Richard paid special attention to Emma himself and looked on approvingly as her cousins and friends were so solicitous.

"Some people think you have to grow in to Bach," said Don. "I don't think it is an acquired taste. The girls enjoyed it." They smiled confirmation. "The same goes for jazz – though not so much as for Bach – I used to be told off by my parents for listening to jazz on the American Forces Network late at night. Give things a chance and you'll find riches."

"True," said Dewey. "What were you talking about?"

"Jazz and Bach," said Kate helpfully.

"I like Bach – not much jazz. It's my sense of form."

"They're getting ready for the second half," observed Ophelia. "Shall we go back?" She looked to her cousin, who nodded. "Yes."

"This is for you," said Richard as he passed Don, who looked around as though for his present. It was Django Reinhardt's "Nuages", cleverly arranged for violin, flute and piano. More Bach followed: the sarabande from the French suite number three in B minor, cool beauty which the pianist clearly relished. The next two pieces they played as a trio: "September Song" and "Polly's Song" from "The Threepenny Opera".

"Are you enjoying Kurt Weill, Don?" asked Emma, leaning across; she knew the answer. The flautist played the famous song from "Singapore" by Sahir Ludhianvi and S. D. Burman: "This night, this moonlight may never be ours again. Heed the story of my heart." The girls did not know the words but were making the most of the evening, conscious that time was running out. There would have been more of Kuala Lumpur, had there been less of Thailand.

The violinist struck up Franz Lehar's "The Merry Widow Waltz" and the others in turn joined in. It was a wistful end to Richard's last recital yet a joyous anticipation of reunion with his waltz-loving wife.

"The students will miss you," said Hazel. He seemed unsure how to answer her as he stood up and hurried to congratulate the performers, urging them to take a second bow – and a third. Don wanted to speak to them too, telling them of the six different versions of "Nuages" and offering the opinion that Django's electric guitar recordings are inferior to his best work.

"Not a patch on them" agreed the violinist, the one who had heard most of the Hot Club of France. so aptly named for the climate of Kuala Lumpur.

"It's a pity I don't have room for you to give recitals," regretted Don. "Are patrons always in short supply?" The flautist nodded ruefully.

"They are," said Richard, "but I can put the word about. And people who've heard you here can vouch for your talent." That cheered them up as they went to take their well-earned refreshments.

"Are you leaving in the morning, James?" asked Dewey.

"Yes. I must away to Australia."

"Is life speeding up," asked Don, "now that you'll have money for research – and, if necessary, publication? Your book's nearer each day."

"I feel better than I did a few weeks ago."

"In that case, you're going to enjoy yourself," announced Dewey.

"I'll fetch my records," said Don, who had left them in a smaller sitting room.

"Will you miss all this, Richard?" asked Emma.

"I've spent much of my life travelling on business. This has not been altogether my home; I've been a visitor, like Hazel. It's only now I'm retiring that I'll settle down. Perhaps we were both born to be globetrotters."

"Are we?" asked Kate.

"I doubt it. Travellers, yes. Some people seem destined to be ex-patriates. I can't picture myself in England now. Australia could be a halfway house."

Don reappeared, with his record player; the girl who liked Django Reinhardt had insisted on carrying his records.

"Just there, thanks. Go and have something to eat; you'll still have time to join in." With a last glance at a record cover, she obeyed.

"Andy wants me to dance with him," said Emma with trepidation. "I don't feel up to it."

"I'll tire him out," promised Dewey. She looked around for him and James, who was talking to Hazel and three other women.

"He's being lionised," said Don, "and his book hasn'tbeen published yet" He started with a Sinatra record as Dewey singled out James for her warm-up and Andy came over to talk to the girls.

"Travel broadens the mind. Can you feel the breadth?"

"I'm not Humpty-Dumpty," declared Kate, "but I do enjoy travel."

"I'd keep away from America if I were you."

"I am me, so I shall."

"Remember George," murmured Ophelia.

"I will." Kate's face clouded, thinking of his untimely death.

"I'll sit this out," said Emma, approached by Andy, pleading her drink.

"James is blossoming," observed Kate, not used to seeing the scholar so relaxed. Don, who liked plenty of humour in his life, was enjoying the dancers between selecting records.

"Dewey's learned new steps," said Ophelia.

"She has a fund of steps. A thousand and thirty-nine steps."

"Kate, you must say good-bye to Kuala Lumpur with a flourish," declared Andy; and she was in his arms. Richard suggested that Hazel take the floor. "My dancing days are over," she declared.

"Something stately for Hazel," said Emma, turning over records. "A pavane."

"Not a pavane in sight," regretted Don.

"No Ravel. No Fauré. Slow foxtrot?"

"Do you have a Kuala Lumpur wardrobe that you wear when winter is getting you down?" asked Emma.

"A Kuala Lumpur jumper," said Don to himself.

"It won't be winter this time. When it is dismal, I wear brighter clothes and jewellery that cheers me up – not always from here though. I'd better speak to those people before they go." They waited for her. Richard turned to Ophelia.

"Do you think you could ever fall in love with the city as Hazel has done?"

"Probably not. Hazel feels Kuala Lumpur was waiting for her from the day she was born. She just had to find it."

Did it occur to Emma that she just had to find George? Now he was gone.

"I'd better say some good-byes too," decided Richard, speaking to James on the way after dodging Andy and Kate and wishing the girl violinist well as she returned after a bite to eat, drawn by music that was new to her. Don passed her a Sinatra record. "You can read the sleeve notes?" She could.

"Dewey has found a tango – she's full of surprises. Just one, and it's short – a short tango in Kuala Lumpur."

"What is it?"

"Vous Permettez, Monsieur?", by Salvatore Adamo. She assures me that it was a big hit in Chile. I never knew Dewey was Chilean."

James broke off dancing, pleading an early start and time needed to sort out his luggage – Richard thought he could find a buyer for some gems.

"I've enjoyed your company," said James to his partner, Don and Ophelia, looking for a chance to say good-bye to the whirling Andy and Kate.

"Give them a wave," advised Don. "You need to get away."

Kate, seeing Dewey free, sensed freedom for herself and bounced off Andy towards her friends. "What's Andy dancing?" asked Don.

"Not the same as me."

"Kate's a good sport," said her sister. Kate grimaced.

"Are you going to play the tango?" asked the violinist.

"Next but one," promised Don. "Let Andy and Dewey get in to the swing of things, then they'll feel the tango."

"It won't be on long enough," objected Ophelia.

"You're probably right." It was short but they enjoyed the humour and charm. Dewey unleashed her tango with a panache they admired.

"Is he French?" asked Emma, "With that name?"

"Dewey says that he was born in Sicily; the family moved to Belgium when he was a year old. The great singer-songwriters are mostly southerners or foreigners."

"I like him," said Emma. "So do I. Encore?"

"Yes. Hazel looks as if she's getting ready to leave. I must say good-bye."

"I'll come with you," said Kate, "before Andy grabs me again."

"Save the tango for when I come back," instructed Emma.

"Dewey has some more songs," he enticed.

Hazel was chatting about Las Vegas and New York, which she had liked as a change from Kuala Lumpur. She had found her personal paradise.

"I thought my last visit would be the last but it wasn't. I may not see K.L. again but I live in hope."

"Aren't you dancing?" Richard asked Kate.

"I was. I may have another go. I enjoy the music. Andy was champing at the bit to dance with Dewey."

"He enjoyed dancing with you," assured Emma. "I could see that he did. You weren't second best."

"I am on a dance floor." Richard looked inquiringly at Emma to see if her cousin lacked confidence. Hazel thought differently:

"You're a lovely girl, and bright, but you should not be so headstrong. There. I thought I'd better say it before I go."

"I've rationed myself to one glass of wine."

"Sensible," approved her cousin. "Did Don pour it for you?"

"Yes. It wasn't up to the brim. I'll go and see how my sister's getting on," letting Hazel know that she could be responsible.

Headstrong? Me? thought Kate as she circumvented the dancers.

"It's unfair," said Don, "but Andy puts me in mind of Sir Andrew Aguecheek."

"Mm." A twinkle in Ophelia's eyes showed she could see his point. "He's masterful, but he is funny."

"I'm glad someone else thinks so."

"Will you go back to England?"

"I'm used to being warm. You mean, when I retire. I'll cross that bridge when I come to it. In the meantime, my expertise is in South East Asia; so is Andy's – I think. Emma could teach in many places."

"Here's Kate. Are you getting on the horse again?"

"Andy would rock me off. Hazel has just called me headstrong."

"Why ever would she think that?" wondered her sister.

"Odd," agreed Don. "Has Emma been bucked up by the music?"

Kate thought back to her cousin's demeanour. "Maybe."

"We should buy her a couple of Adamo C.D.s," said Ophelia.

"We'll ask Dewey's advice and look on line."

"Not long now," reflected Kate. "We'll soon be on the way home.

We've met some likeable, interesting people. Will you miss us, Don?",

"I feel like Treebeard rejuvenated by meeting the Hobbits."

"We're not like Hobbits," protested Kate. "We don't have hairy feet."

"Emma's coming over," observed Ophelia.

"With Hazel?"

"No. Not yet." Richard seemed to be confiding in Hazel yet no-one was near.

"I've enjoyed the evening," said Emma," but I don't have the energy of Dewey. Dance with me, Don, if Andy looks like asking me. You're my pace."

"Is Hazel leaving tomorrow, like James?" asked Kate.

"She is. Here she comes to say good-bye to you."

"It's been a pleasure to meet you," said the stalwart of Kuala Lumpur. Hazel hugged Emma, Kate, Ophelia and, for good measure, the violinist.

"I like Richard's idea. He'll tell you about it." She left them guessing.

"I hope we'll see you here again," was Don's valediction. Andy and Dewey broke off dancing to wish her well. Emma was studying Richard, who had an idea.

"Time for a cup of tea," decided Andy. "Would you like that, Dewey, or something stronger?"

"Tea for me."

"Emma? The rest of you?" He speedily returned with a tray and Richard on his heels. Their host was beaming.

"I'd like you and your cousins to come to stay with me and my wife for a few days. We're going to live near Melbourne but we have a holiday home in wooded hills to the north. Don't worry about school. Dewey has persuaded the principal to give you an extra week's leave."

"Well done, Dewey," exclaimed Don.

Kate was quick to react: "We think you should accept."

"You should," replied Emma, "but don't your parents expect you home? I thought I'd be able to relax when you were safely on the plane."

"We came from Singapore unchaperoned."

"And look what happened."

"We can't go without you," coaxed Ophelia.

"It will do them good and you good," insisted Andy.

"Why not celebrate with a dance?" invited Don. "The tango." Emma took the floor at last and took the eye. The length of a tango she forgot her sorrows.

"You're more than ready for Australia after south-east Asia," said Andy. "I hope you don't find it dull."

"Lazing on beaches," mused Kate. "No Red Shirts or C.I.A."

"You've learned more than you would from a politics degree."

Kate felt pleased that Andy thought they had gone a little way towards acquiring his savoir-faire and knowledge of the world; it was a start. She was even inclined to dance with him again.

"Have you played the two on the other side?" she asked the violinist, who had been left in charge by Don.

"Not yet." As the record ended, she looked at the other titles, turning them over in her mind as though that would be a clue to the sound.

"There's one with a Javanese rhythm," said Dewey, "but I don't have that."

"Birds of paradise live in New Guinea. Are there bowerbirds in Australia?" asked Ophelia.

"Yes, but far to the north," answered Richard. Robinson Crusoe, in his bower, never saw bowerbirds.

Emma returned to her expectant cousins.

"Have you made up your mind?" asked Kate. "If we're going to Australia. It will have to be soon. The day after tomorrow?"

"Take in another continent," exhorted Andy. "Make it a Grand Tour."

"A flying visit yet a Grand Tour," summed up Don. "You haven't been here long but it has been eventful – and I haven't witnessed all your adventures."

"Let's hear the other side" proposed Emma, keeping them on tenterhooks. Andy danced with the violinist, rounding off a memorable evening for her. Emma was looking cheerful.

"Australia's the place for coloured diamonds," recalled Richard.

"I'm glad my wife's not keen on diamonds; she prefers cheaper gems. "

Leaving Don to play a last Sinatra record, Emma turned to her cousins.

"We ought to go to Australia while we're so near," reasoned Kate.

"Near? A few thousand miles. If your parents approve, yes. You won't be able to afford a gap year, will you?"

"No," regretted Kate.

"So the memories of this trip will have to last you a long time. Make the most of it. Cheer up, Kate. It need not be the trip of a lifetime. Where's Richard when you want to accept?" She went looking for him. He was seeing off another guest.

"Don," exclaimed Kate excitedly, "Emma told me to cheer up."

"Good. We're on to something, Dewey."

"We want things that don't shout: "Kuala Lumpur", said Kate, shopping next day. "They should whisper exotic quality – and not be too expensive."

"You mean: they should not be souvenirs but you want things you can't easily buy in England." Emma made clear to herself what they were after.

"They'll be souvenirs to us though," said Ophelia. Emma ducked her head, more in thought than nodding, then led them to the first of several shops she thought up to their requirements and down to their budgets. Pleased with their purchases, they headed for the coffee house.

"Will a shower in late afternoon always remind you of Kuala Lumpur?" asked Emma. They had sheltered in a shop.

"Probably," replied Kate. "We may not know what else until we get home."

"Is it going ahead?" asked Dewey.

"Yes. I said it would be educational; Richard is of irreproachable character and great experience and I'll be there. And we're not going near crocodiles,. Their father had heard that you should zig-zag when chased."

"Wouldn't work," said Dewey. "Don't you hit sharks on the nose?"

"In extremis. I wouldn't advise you to hit sharks on the nose, Dewey."

As he gave this advice, Don slipped a sheet of paper in to Dewey's hand.

Emma was looking towards the counter. Her cousins were intrigued.

"I need a napkin," said Emma. "This is sticky. Would anyone like more coffee while I'm there?"

Dewey would. Ophelia fancied hot chocolate for a change. Dewey was particular about her coffee.

"What's it about?" asked Kate.

"Kuala Lumpur and Singapore are known for entrepreneurs," explained Don. "We want one who'll send two Adamo C.D.s to Melbourne post haste."

"Or up country," added Dewey. "Whichever they can manage?"asked Ophelia.

"We have Andy working at it," went on Don, "He knows more businessmen than we do." Emma had paid and was returning with her napkin, followed by a waitress with a tray of drinks.

"Can you download them?" asked Kate.

"We're not of the ephemeral generation. I'm not. Is Emma, Dewey?"

"No. She enjoys reading sleeve notes and looking at photographs. A record's something in your hand. Like a book."

"I agree," said Emma, hearing the last words. "Chocolate, Ophelia. I think the coffee will meet your specifications, Dewey. You're more particular than usual."

"Here's Andy," said Kate, recognising him beyond a group of Malaysians. She tried not to look too excited. Was Emma to be kept in the dark until they were sure of the gift?

"I'm looking forward to drawing Australia," said Ophelia to Emma. "I promised Hazel drawings of Kuala Lumpur; I'll have to send her some from Victoria." Dewey folded the sheet of paper and put it in her purse.

"That will be a pleasant surprise for her," said Emma. "It should be peaceful in Australia – as far as anywhere is nowadays."

"Has Australia been involved in the kidnapping of suspected terrorists?"

"Maybe not," answered Don. "Some information about the second world war only came out much later. Russians who had lived in the west for twenty-five years were handed over to Stalin. An army officer was asked for his word as an English officer and gentleman that the train wasn't bound for the Soviet Union. He was ordered to lie."

Ophelia shook her head at such iniquity..

"The forced repatriation of Russians continued until General Eisenhower stopped it on his own initiative."

"The President?"

"Yes. President in the 'fifties."

"Andy," asked Kate. "Is all going well with your negotiations?"

"Well enough. People are being helpful. What would you recommend today, Dewey?" She took the hint and accompanied him to the counter.

"Do you know a coffee house as good as this in England?" asked Don.

"I can think of one."

"Where you take your sketch book? Or just overhear conversations?"

"You enjoy that."

"I'm a journalist – of sorts."

As Dewey came back, she whispered to Don: "Two C.D.s; they'll be sent up country. We have both addresses."

"And they're early? Youthful? Spring-like?" She nodded.

"Glad to be of help," said Andy. To the girls: "You've packed plenty in to the trip. I hope we'll see you here again."

"It's the people we'll remember," said Kate, "even more than the places."

Ophelia guessed who was in Kate's mind but said nothing.

"I'm old-fashioned," said Emma. "1 don't carry a lap-top all the time but I wouldn't mind being able to take this coffee house with me."

"You're not going away yet, not far," said Don softly.

"No. Not yet. I like it here, I'll know when it's time to try somewhere else."

They lingered as long as they could with needing to pack.

"From Don," said Emma in the morning, disclosing a record of Django Reinhardt, "and from Dewey," two very Chinese silk scarves, which would have cost a fortune in the West. Dewey knew where to look.

Thirty-six hours later, they boarded the train from Melbourne, marveling at Andy's contacts – except – why one? was Kate's thought.
"You like the record?" Emma smiled. "I love his voice."
"There's another. They've split the order: one to each house."
"They can't get everything right," defended Ophelia.
"I'm sure I'll enjoy it as much. I'll go and see what Richard has found in the dining car. They could be serving a hot meal."
Kate watched the suburbs turning to farmland then to woods.
"We began our story on a train."
"Not the journey."
"But the story, the adventure. And we're ending it on a train."
"There's more to our stay in Australia yet."